Other books by
DOUGLAS GLOVER

The Mad River

Precious

Dog Attempts to Drown Man in Saskatoon

The South Will Rise at Noon

A Guide to Animal Behaviour

The Life and Times of Captain N.

Notes Home from a Prodigal Son

16
Categories
of Desire

stories by

DOUGLAS GLOVER

GOOSE LANE

Edited by Laurel Boone.
Cover: *In the Temple of Freedom* (detail) copyright © Carol Kennedy, 1998.
Cover and interior design by Julie Scriver.
Printed in Canada by Transcontinental.
10 9 8 7 6 5 4 3 2 1

Canadian Cataloguing in Publication Data

Glover, Douglas, 1948-
16 categories of desire

ISBN 0-86492-314-7

I. Title. II. Title: Sixteen categories of desire.

PS8563.L64S59 2000   C813'.54   C00-901010-6
PR9199.3.G584S59 2000

Published with the financial support of the Canada Council for the Arts,
the Government of Canada through the Book Publishing Industry
Development Program, and the New Brunswick Culture and Sports Secretariat.

Goose Lane Editions
469 King Street
Fredericton, New Brunswick
CANADA E3B 1E5

This book is for my dog Nellie

Contents

SIXTEEN CATEGORIES OF DESIRE

La Corriveau

I

I WAKE UP THE NEXT MORNING in my little rented tourist flat on rue des Ramparts with a really terrible headache and a strange dead man in bed next to me.

First, let me tell you that nothing like this has ever happened to me before.

In bed with a dead man — never.

Often they may have seemed dead. You know — limp, moribund, unimaginative, sleepy or just drunk to the point of oblivion. But until now I have avoided actual morbidity in my lovers.

I resist an initial impulse to interpret his sudden and surprising fatality as an implicit critique of our lovemaking the night before.

To tell the truth I don't remember our lovemaking, but the man and I are naked and the sheets are in wild disarray and I am a bit sore here and there, which leads me to draw certain embarrassing conclusions.

Embarrassing because I don't remember any of this and especially his name or anything else about him.

He is clearly dead and naked. And a man. Beyond this I know nothing (although, with his sinewy slimness, protuberant eyes and thick lips, he bears a strong resemblance to Mick Jagger, the man of my dreams).

To tell the truth, it makes me a little panicky being in bed with a corpse (however handsome) and feeling that I might be held responsible for him at some point, when in all honesty I can't say that I have ever seen him before in my life, though our having had intimate relations before, and quite possibly after, his demise seems indubitable.

Briefly, I entertain the sanguine fantasy that this is a joke, that my lover possesses a sick sense of humour which lends itself to overly prolonged impersonations of dead people. Perhaps this is some sort of weird sex game. I laugh lightheartedly and pinch his earlobe as hard as I can. It is cold as ice and stiffish to the touch.

Dead.

I jump out of bed with a shiver of disgust.

At least, I think, he didn't get up and leave in the middle of the night the way most men do.

On the other hand, our breakfast conversation is going to be a little one-sided.

In the bathroom, I pee and splash cold water on my cheeks to promote circulation. I look everywhere for some aspirin but find none. My hair is a nest of tangles on top of my head, and there is something, possibly chewing gum, stuck in the back. (What *did* we do last night?) My breasts look bruised and tiny — androgynous is one word for my chest. I am so tall I have to stoop to see my face in the mirror above the sink. Once a man told me I had the figure of a Yugoslavian volleyball star. I don't think it was the man in the bed, but it might have been.

When I return to the bedroom, he is still there (I had had hopes he would disappear, that I had been dreaming or hallucinating).

I think, a girl comes to Quebec for a little winter carnival fun and the next thing she knows a dead man gets into bed with her and ruins her vacation. I should complain to the Ministry of Tourism — anonymously, of course, and from home when I get there.

His eyes are open, little brown gelid globes. I have a weakness for brown eyes and men with accents. I realize now he must be French and am briefly fearful of the constitutional implications, me

being English-speaking and from Toronto; I can see the headlines:
ANGLO TOURIST SLAYS INNOCENT QUÉBECOIS FAMILY MAN
IN FATAL SEX ORGY.

The French are so sensitive these days.

I recall his name suddenly — Robert. Not actually recall, but
there is a work shirt draped over the chair, one of the kind garage
mechanics and delivery men wear, with their first names stitched
above the breast pocket, and the name over the pocket is Robert.

Poor Robert.

Dead for love. Heart attack, I think, or anaphylactic shock
brought on by eating shellfish. (Had we eaten shellfish before
making love? I make a mental note to look in the kitchen trash.)

But then I notice the dark stain on the sheet beneath him, the
spillage on the fire-resistant carpet next to the bed and the Swiss
Army pocket knife (mine, I am forced to admit — a gift from a
former lover obsessed with outdoor pursuits) protruding from his
ribs just beneath his shoulder blade.

My headache is suddenly worse, possibly the penumbral over-
ture to a full-blown migraine. Also, I am extremely irritated with
Robert for inflicting his personal problems on me like this, first
thing in the morning before my shower and a cup of coffee. I make
up my mind then and there not to let this spoil the rest of my time
in Quebec (a mere three-day weekend, a third of which is already
gone).

Briskly, I form a plan and put it into action, grasping Robert by
his ankles (slim, handsome ankles, unlike my unfeminine tree
trunks) and dragging him out to the tiny balcony overlooking the
river and Lévis, on the far shore, shrouded in a brilliant icy mist.

I recall reading in a tourist brochure how drovers once herded
cattle across the frozen river to the abattoirs of Quebec and how, if
you see a man's severed head upon the ice, it is a sign you will
shortly die. Had Robert seen a head upon the ice? If so, I don't
believe he mentioned it to me.

(On the whole, I find it disturbing that the people who write these brochures seem to think that tourists will be interested in such bloody and lugubrious bits of information. How strange, dark and tortured the Québecois mind seems when you begin to examine it closely, how obsessed with death, separation, the loss of memory — they have that motto *Je me souviens,* which I translate loosely as "I remember myself" — and hydro-electric power. I leave you with this thought free of charge for what it's worth.)

I arrange my silent lover in a plastic patio chair, his arms crossed on the balcony railing and his chin nestled against his forearms, and drape his shoulders with a blanket, so he looks like a man enjoying the view.

Then I strip the soiled sheets and replace them with fresh ones and bathe and dress in jeans and mukluks and an oversized duffel coat, which must have been Robert's, for I neglected myself to bring anything so eminently suited to the climate.

I trudge through the fresh accumulation of snow along rue Port-Dauphin past many stately and historic buildings made of grey stone, thinking apropos of nothing that the tourist's lot is a lonely one, and also about Hélène Boullé (also lonely, also a sort of tourist) who married Samuel de Champlain, founder of Quebec, in 1610 when he was forty and she was twelve. How jolly for him, I think, somewhat acerbically.

She came to Canada in 1620 but had a difficult time adjusting to life in the New World and returned to France four years later. When her husband died in 1635, she entered a convent under the name of Sister Hélène de Saint-Augustin.

This is a sad little story which reminds me of my own. Like Hélène Boullé, I have had a difficult time adjusting to life in Canada, though, unlike her, I have nowhere else to go.

This present contretemps — Robert, clearly a victim of murder, showing up indiscreetly in my bed — is merely another instance of a bizarre and insidious synchronicity that has dogged me from the beginning.

I am thirty-seven years old (Hélène Boullé-Champlain's age

when she entered the convent), a poet and office temp, unmarried (unless you count my twelve-year affair with an already-attached CBC radio producer named Edward, now aging and paunchy) and desperate. Also prone to fainting, blackouts, syncopes and blinding migraines — I have been advised to take stress-management instruction.

Oh yes, I have given everything for my art, just as Robert has given everything, including his jacket, for love, just as Hélène Champlain-de Saint Augustin, née Boullé, gave everything for God. (Or have I missed something?)

We are people of extremes, a nation within a nation, without language or identity.

At a bookstore called Librairie Garneau in Place d'Armes, I buy a book of Quebec military history (more death and defeat — whatever you say about them, they are a people of poetry) and two newspapers (in French — unreadable). Then I slip through an alley to a café overlooking Parc des Gouverneurs, where I sit next to a window and order a croissant and a cappuccino.

It occurs to me that someone ought to be alerted to Robert's condition, that an investigation should take place. But then I think of the bother, the questions, the searching interrogations, which might reveal — what? — more than I care to say about myself. For example, my dismal poetry career, my love for Mick Jagger, certain bizarre sexual preferences that point to childhood abuse (of which I have no memory).

I have surprisingly little curiosity about the actual events of the previous night, suspecting, perhaps with reason, that it was all too, too humiliating for words.

Across from me, in the little park, there are snow and ice sculptures representing mythological and folkloric figures, figures of dream or nightmare. But no severed heads or death-driven cattle. No statue to Hélène Boullé, perhaps the first woman to speak her mind in Canadian history.

(One can imagine the scene: Dead of winter, wind howling

through the chinks in the log walls, a miserly fire glowing on the hearth, Hélène wrapped in coarse wool and animal skins, sneezing and coughing between sentences.

Hélène: M. Champlain, I don't like it here.

Samuel: But it's lovely. And the savages are really nice once you get to know them. And why do you keep calling me M. Champlain?

Hélène: I hate it. No one ever asked me if I wanted to come. I was playing with my dolly, Jehan, and they told me I was to be married. And then I was married and you went away for ten years. And now look, you're very old and I'm not having fun.)

I feel suddenly claustrophobic, as if I have wakened to find myself immured behind the stone walls of a convent. (Do I hear police sirens in the distance, trailing along the walls of this medieval city, founded first for greed and then for God — poor Jacques Cartier, when he got back to France and discovered his diamonds were quartz?) My mind is wandering. My headache . . . well.

Suddenly, I recall horses and a carriage and a nighttime ride with a man who seemed, with his horsewhip, duffel coat and French accent, the very image of romance, a boreal Mick Jagger.

But what did we do with the horse? (Now I do detect a distinctive equine odour on my coat.)

I believe things are coming back to me.

This leads me to rush off, leaving my coffee cold (as Robert), my croissant untouched, my newspapers unread (what could possibly be new?). Movement seems imperative to ward off the flood of memories which just might possibly prove unpleasant if not actually inculpatory.

There are still few people about on account of the extremely low temperature and the generally threatening nature of the weather. The place is as hospitable to human habitation as Mars. (Oh Canada, our home and alien land.)

No wonder Hélène Boullé hated it.

Then I have a jarring thought. What if history is a male lie? What if she actually loved Canada, and Samuel sent her back because he was envious? What if she was having too good a time, the Indians loved her, she found the savage religions appealing, she was beginning to take their side in beaver trade disputes?

Perhaps she never got to speak her mind, do what she wanted to do.

And when Samuel died and she went meekly like a lamb into the convent, did she even know what she thought?

Did she remember?

Je me souviens is a difficult motto to live up to; I myself remember nothing.

I circle back past the funicular, following the city walls again, till I stand just opposite my darling little flat (with kitchenette and sitting room and Sacred Heart bleeding above the bedstead, all for an extremely reasonable price). Robert, a.k.a. Mick, is still peering out at the steaming river and the ice-rimed, smoking buildings of Lévis on the far shore, though the snow is beginning to drift a little behind him and he has an odd-looking triangular cap upon his head.

What do his dead eyes see? I ask myself. Figures of ice and floating heads?

Does he hear the lurid song of La Corriveau, the Siren of Quebec (see those tourist brochures), who murdered her husband and was hanged and exposed in an iron cage above a crossroads till her body rotted? (Later the cage became a minor exhibit in Mr. Barnum's circus — you can make whatever you want of this outré fact.)

Did I dream this, or did Robert? A naked woman running, slipping in the snow. La Corriveau, to be sure. Calling for help, calling the men of the city to their deaths.

(This is the legend, at any rate, that she returns from time to time, attracts men with her pitiable lamentations, then slaughters them. To my mind, she is just crabby, just a little premenstrual, if you know what I mean, because the whole thing was such a mess, what with the cage being built too short and her having to crouch even after they hanged her, a victim of incompetent male technocrats. Ugh!)

I think of the great and saintly Bishop Laval who died here three hundred years ago after suffering frostbite on his bare feet doing penance in the snow.

Oh Quebec (as a poet, I am an aficionado of the rhetorical device called apostrophe), death-driven, poetical, and strange. (The obsession with hydroelectric power, dams and rivers seems symptomatic of a mother complex — in the throes of passion, did not dear Robert call out for his church and for his mother, or possibly his horse? Am I making this up? Or am I merely, like all English Canadians, obsessed with dissecting my French other — my mother calls them Kew-beckers?)

2

I AM WRITING my confession down — I might as well let you know — under the grey stare of a police detective who tells me his name is Gilbert and who has once or twice interrupted my narrative to tell me amusing anecdotes about his children and his wife, whom he insists on calling "ma blonde."

He resembles Mick Jagger somewhat, though perhaps it is only the black leather bomber jacket he wears that gives me this impression.

Gilbert particularly wants me to explain the presence of my Swiss Army knife in the interstices of Robert's ribs. He calls this knife "the cause of death," a summary designation which I find reductive and unpoetical.

If Robert had not been born, he surely would not have died, I say, remembering (as usual) nothing, feeling the iron bars of the cage squeezing inward on my brain. Yes, my headache has not abated.

The police found the horse, it seems, wandering in the streets before dawn, dragging its empty carriage, suffering frostbite and loneliness.

From time to time, she would lift her head and whinny plaintively for Robert to take her home.

Her name is Nellie, and she is now in police custody.

When Gilbert tells me this story, I break down and weep.

I have seduced a man into betraying his horse.

(With this, I remember again my solitary midnight ride among the ice sculptures, the fantastic, contorted shapes, all lit up and glowing. I recall Robert, duffel-coated and masterful, wrapping me in blankets and guiding the horse with clucks of his tongue.)

Gilbert peers over my shoulder and clucks his tongue sympathetically. Perhaps I would like a cup of coffee, he says. Perhaps some other refreshment, a change of air.

His English is only adequate, I think. But charming. His eyes are brown. When we stand, his head reaches to my shoulder, but I feel certain he has enough self-esteem not to be bothered by the physical discrepancy.

Even so I crouch a little as we walk.

He takes me to a café a block from the police station and orders a cappuccino and a brioche.

I tell him of my memory lapses (a common Anglo-Canadian complaint), my language problems, my blackouts and my inability to find a publisher for my poetry.

Somewhat irritatingly, he keeps trying to steer the conversation back to Robert, who is a dead letter as far as I am concerned, a character to be written out of the story.

I tell Gilbert he reminds me of Mick Jagger.

He smiles and lights a cigarette and tells me I too remind him of someone, a woman he saw in a dream.

Uh-oh, I think.

I say, I suppose you assume I'm the sort of girl who travels around preying on French-Canadian calèche drivers named Robert.

He gives a throaty, Mick Jaggerish chuckle, and I can see right away that we have established a relationship that goes beyond the purely professional, that he sees me as someone other than the run-of-the-mill murderess, someone who perhaps needs a protecting arm.

A tiny muscle in my neck begins to pulse like a second heart.

There are snow-covered statues at either end of the street, resembling the icy sculptures in the Old Town, tortured, demonic creatures, visions of some frigid Hell.

My headache is worse, a virtual blazing light of pain, as though my skull were caught in the bars of a cage.

I realize suddenly that my infatuation with Mick Jagger is merely an extension of English Canada's pernicious anglophilia — substitute the Queen for Mick and I am like anyone else from Saskatoon or Victoria.

To cover my discomfiture, I tell Gilbert the story (culled from inane and ubiquitous tourist brochures) of Marie de l'Incarnation, an early religious pioneer in New France, who (like me) had visions and was married twice and who, in 1631, entered the Ursuline convent at Tours despite the pleadings of her only son, who stood outside the doors screaming, "Give me back my mother."

On the whole, I think, French-Canadian history is littered with dysfunctional families. It is difficult to know what to make of this fact.

Gilbert has a tear in his eye. I have touched him with my little tale. He understands, as any member of his race would, that all life is either metonymic or synecdochic. The policeman in him is at war with the poet. It is refreshing to see such passion in a public servant.

We warm to each other in the humid little café, despite the cold front descending on the city beyond the windows. People walking in the streets take on the aspect of ice statues. Ice statues begin to resemble ordinary tourists, shoppers and dead calèche drivers.

Night is falling, despite my impression that day just dawned moments ago.

Gilbert says that at first they thought Robert had frozen to death. Only after he thawed out did they discover the knife wound.

I remember nothing, I say.

They found me at the city zoo, which specializes in native species now extinct in southern Ontario where I live. (There are, for example, cages full of Native Americans, Anglo Poets, Entirely Free Women, Liberated Men and Innocent Children.)

I think, how I long for the time when the black bear and moose will return to the tepid streets of Toronto.

Gilbert leans forward, his face pregnant with pity and empathy, and touches my wrist with the tips of his fingers. He wishes to tell me that he is not a projection of my dreams, that he is himself, separate and whole, and that he will help me if I let him.

I remember nothing, I say.

But his gentleness disarms me. All at once, I begin to weep. It is clear that I have gotten off on the wrong foot with this man, that there is still gum in my hair, that when I left the flat this morning I put on the same clothes I wore the day before, that killing Robert was a monumental faux pas. (My constant reference to loss of memory in the foregoing is clearly a case of reaction formation; we all try to put our worst crimes in the best light possible.)

All I can say in my defence is that homicide is totally out of character for me, most days.

Gilbert suggests a calèche ride. Perhaps we might attempt to recapitulate the events of the evening before so as to jog my memory.

Meekly, I assent.

(I think, soon now my lifelong fantasy of being hung above a crossroads to rot, in full public view, will become a reality.)

Through the testimony of witnesses who saw me in Robert's carriage, the police have been able to reconstruct much of our route.

The driver is a non-French-speaking Irish exchange student named Reilly.

The horse's name is Retribution. (I mention this, though quite possibly it is an unimportant detail.)

In moments we emerge from the Porte Saint-Louis and turn down Avenue George VI into the former battlefield (now rolling parkland). A gusty wind drives swirls of ice particles round the lampposts and into our faces. Gilbert and I huddle together, wrapped in a five-point Hudson Bay trading blanket.

Here, as everywhere else, city officials have erected myriad ice statues commemorating significant events in the nation's history. Behind us, the city walls are illuminated, shrieks from revellers and bobsled riders pierce the night air, the funicular rises and falls like breath. But here, Iroquois warriors stalk unwary habitants, Jacques Cartier is mining diamonds along the river shore, Abraham is herding his cows and planting cabbages, and a sickly Wolfe is climbing a narrow path, surrounded by his intrepid, kilted soldiers, with death in his heart.

At the centre of the park, we reach the place of memory (where I believe Robert kissed me for the first time).

I can see by the horrified look on Gilbert's face that he can see what I see — the ice statues come alive, wounded soldiers piled in heaps, dying generals, weeping savages, fatherless children, widows touching themselves in ecstasies of loneliness.

I say to him, I am guilty. Of everything. I wanted to sleep with my father. I poured boiling water into the goldfish bowl when I was eight. I began to masturbate at twelve. I killed Robert the calèche driver (though I fully believe that, after an evening with me, he wanted to die).

I do not say that any of this is trivial, but I shall plead extenuating circumstances. I shall blame history, lurid tourist brochures and love gone wrong.

This time I'll get off, I say. You'll see.

I do not think he hears me.

My Romance

OUR BOY NEDDY DIED when he was three months old. I hardly remember any of this except for the brief hours following his birth when we were a normal, happy couple and then afterwards when Annie would wake in the night, choked with sobs, her milk seeping through the cloth of her nightgown. "The baby's hungry. He needs to eat," she would whisper, then curl into a tight, convulsive ball, a spasm of despair.

When I heard her weeping, I wondered how anyone could live through such sadness. The look in her wild eyes pleaded with me to save her, to wake her from the nightmare, but all I could think of was holding him those first moments, dancing him a little in the delivery room, peering into his dark blue eyes, crooning, "Neddy, Neddy, Neddy."

Afterwards I stopped sleeping. I forced myself to sit in his nursery with the dinosaur wallpaper, the crib with the delicate white spindles, the Babar poster and the panda bear mobile that played "Twinkle, twinkle, little star" when you wound it up.

I drank neat bourbon, knocked back Valium my doctor had prescribed and smoked cigarettes. Sometimes I would pass out, but I never slept. "My baby is hungry," I heard her whisper. I couldn't go back into our bedroom. The grief drove us apart. We were drowning in separate wells. Neddy had never actually slept in the nursery. The nursery was all future. He slept in our bed, tucked between us. Without saying a word, we both believed we could save him with the power of our love. That's when I stopped sleeping.

Afterwards, in the nursery, I couldn't feel anything; I wondered if feeling would ever come back.

"What are you doing, sweetheart?" she cried once.

I couldn't say. I was surprised she even noticed. I was playing "Twinkle, twinkle, little star," watching the bears and stars circle above the place where Ned would have slept.

She said, "I came to get the baby. I heard him crying. You know I can hear him quite well from the bedroom. He needs me. He needs to be fed."

She smelled sour from the old milk on her nightgown. Her breasts were huge and bountiful and useless. "You shouldn't smoke in here," she said sternly.

"He's dead," I said, sobbing so hard I couldn't catch my breath.

I was so lonely. At the same time, I was envious of her. She had slipped right out of herself into some fantasy. I remembered the afternoon we made Ned, the orange indicator on the ovulation test kit, our single-minded love, the sex without fear, the exhilaration of leaping into the future together. We looked into each other's eyes until I came and my eyelids slid shut and I sank onto her shoulder and she held me. Now, even when we were in the same room talking, we were never together.

Part of me knew we were play-acting, cheering ourselves up. I understood we were performing ancient rituals of grief. At the edge of the abyss you dance or you fall in. I didn't really believe Annie thought she heard Neddy's cries in the night. This was her way of creating drama out of her heartsickness just as drinking bourbon and playing "Twinkle, twinkle, little star" was my way of passing time that was otherwise utterly empty. Neither of us could abide the chilly emptiness we had fallen into, yet neither of us had the least idea how to climb out.

I remembered everything: the first intimations of disaster, the falling weight, Neddy's constant whimpering cry, his bluish pallor, the blue haloes around his eyes, his lassitude, his clammy skin. The doctor had a phrase for this — failure to thrive. She didn't choose the words, they were all she had.

She was young and tall. I had never met anyone I could call willowy before I knew Dr. Tithonous. In better times, in her examining room, she had charmed us with a little dance she did, miming with her hands the finger-like fimbriae harvesting eggs, her undulating body representing the Fallopian tubes. The fimbria dance. When she told us the bad news about Ned, she broke down herself, her long, pale hair fanning out over the cluttered desk as her head went down on her hands.

Annie and I were a little shocked at this show of emotion in a comparative stranger. After all, Annie was holding Neddy on her lap, and he was still alive, if somewhat blue, and we couldn't quite credit the words of this overwrought woman across the desk. She said they called it failure to thrive. But I remembered reading in old books other phrases — mysterious wasting sickness, for example — which seemed more apt, more in tune with the inexplicable nature of things.

It was as if Neddy, having ventured into the world, never quite managed to get a firm grip on existence. His whole short life was an inexorable slipping back. It made you think: What is life and what is death? Is there such a thing as being half-alive, tentatively alive? The darkness spewed him out, then sucked him back as if cancelling an error. I don't think he felt joy — he had a wry, flickering smile that would play across his face from time to time. And his whimpering signalled discomfort, not grief. I sometimes thought it might not have been so bad if he had lived a little, lived in the metaphorical sense — suffered joy and pain, raged and laughed. But he only lingered.

Oddly, the night Neddy died Annie and I both managed to sleep. We cradled his cool body between us on the bed, mashed our hot faces together and wept and wept and then slept. Nature is merciful, I think. They say that small animals go into an anaesthetic shock as predators tear them to pieces. We didn't believe it was over, but something in us knew what had happened and yet briefly allowed us more than the usual fantasy of hope. We were momentarily together in a travesty of the togetherness we had felt a year before, making love, making Neddy.

There was some terrible irony in this which neither of us understood. We could not put names or explanations to the contradictory emotions we felt. With a feeling that was sometimes uncomfortably close to embarrassment, we had lost all sense of who we really were. Everything was tasteless, colourless. Words were meaningless. We told each other "I love you" because we both had a vestigial, somewhat dutiful impulse to comfort one another. We remembered, as if in a dream, that other time when we were really together. But we both also knew these were empty words.

Language is a machine of desire. It works along an axis defined by hope and future. When there is no hope, no imaginable future, the mysterious bonds of syntax, the wires that convey the energy of meaning from word to word, disintegrate. Words become the snarls, shrieks and gurgles of despair or they become rituals, motions you go through to pass the time, to keep your spirits up. If I say "I love you" enough times, perhaps I will remember what that felt like, what the words mean. But the truth is all I remember is how cold Neddy was, lying between us that morning when we woke up and I reached for the telephone to call Dr. Tithonous.

Of course, at that time of day, I only got her service. My voice was breaking. I could barely croak out the words. I said, "Please tell Barbara" — I had never used her first name before — "please tell her Neddy died in the night, that we're here with him in the bed, that we can't leave him, that we don't know what to do now and could she please help us?"

You expect answering service operators to be distant and businesslike at best. But this one seemed, through some miracle of wire and electrons, to understand every nuance of what I was saying. Her voice came back to me full of sorrow and reassurance.

"Sir, I want you to know I will call Dr. Tithonous as soon as you hang up. I'll call her till I find her. I don't want you to worry about this. I'll get someone there right away."

She knew she couldn't help me much, but she wanted me to be sure she would do everything she could. And she didn't offer to do more. She didn't say goodbye.

Almost as soon as I hung up, the phone rang and it was Dr. Tithonous. "I am just calling to let you know I am driving right over myself. I wanted you not to worry."

It broke my heart a second time to have these people trying to take care of us. All the protocols and stereotypes were breaking down. Out of all the wretchedness came the distant mutterings of the human heart. I did not think this then, only later. At the time I simply felt an unreasonable relief and turned to try to cuddle little Neddy one last time, to try to pretend he was alive. And then, moments later, it seemed, I heard the doorbell and stumbled out into the living room in my pyjamas.

Dr. Tithonous embraced me at the door, just held me, for an eternity, it seemed. I felt her dry sobs catch on my ear. Then she let me go and strode quickly into the bedroom. She was wearing faded jeans and a man's shirt not tucked in properly, evidence of her haste in coming. Her hair was still in disarray from sleep. She knelt beside Annie, stroked her hair and whispered to her. I don't know what she said.

Annie had the baby at her breast. Her breasts were bare, distended, ready to burst. Milk had spurted out over the sheets, pooled on her belly. Dr. Tithonous cradled her head and whispered. She touched my wife's breasts, she kissed her temples, she felt the baby's cheek with the back of her hand. At that moment, she seemed to shudder, and she buried her eyes briefly against Annie's shoulder.

I caught sight of myself in Annie's full-length mirror against the closet door. Eyes like dark stones, mouth hanging open. I had an erection, I suddenly noticed. The wild incongruity of this almost drove me to my knees. And I could not think about it then, only thought about it later in my bourbon and Valium stupor, when I could only wonder at the paradoxical messages ripping through my heart, as if I were somehow completely separate from those things called "body" and "self," as if the self I was, or wasn't, was more utterly alien and mysterious than anything I had ever experienced.

At length I crawled into bed with my wife and dead baby, with my erection, in a gross and humiliating parody of the moment of conception, when, yes, we were all together, too. And Dr. Tithonous stayed with us in the death room, in this state of barbaric intimacy.

Weeks later it is like this: I tell Annie I am going to play golf. I don't even bother to put my clubs in the trunk. They sit there in the garage behind the infant car seat neither of us can bear to move or give away. If Annie looked, she would know that I am not playing golf. I don't know if she looks, she never says a word. I just tell her. The Canada geese have come and gone, snow flurries fall — still I head out to play golf with obsessive regularity. What is Annie thinking?

I drive out Route 9 to a little motel called the Royal which climbs up a shattered limestone ridge and hangs in a state of instability and tension with the scrub pine, sumac and poison ivy tumbling down the steep slopes. Dr. Tithonous meets me there when she can break away from her patients. I wait for her in one of the guest cottages, sipping Old Crow. Sometimes I fall asleep. The guest cottages at the Royal are the only place I can sleep these days. Often I waken to find Barbara tucked up beside me wearing nothing but her bra and underpants, her cell phone and beeper placed neatly upon the bedside table next to the lamp.

What happens next is difficult to relate. One's deepest desires are always paradoxical and humiliating. You go there as into some dark vortex at the bottom of which is death, which seems, in this aspect, breathtakingly sweet. Or put it this way: sex is inextricably entwined with desire, with wanting, but what we want is not always sex. Sometimes we desire pure desire, the endless wanting whose only end is the extinction of itself, that point of voluptuous rest from wanting. Or we crave some replica of the utter desperation of life, the way it eats itself up, the self-destructiveness of it all. So it is all desperate, whispered entreaties, whimpered protests, grunts, moans and cries in the dark. I can guess why I am there, but what secret sadness drives Barbara to the Royal Motel I cannot tell. I cannot connect the dancer who showed us with her body the ancient processes of conception with the lover who begs me to perform the most unseemly acts, who only cries out for rest so that she can reach some stranger ecstasy.

Once she told me the story of her life, how she had married another doctor named East, how he left her the year he did eight ultrasounds on a pregnant woman and missed the fact that her baby had no brain, how the year Dr. East left Barbara's twin sister Miranda died of leukemia. Near the end, Barbara came often to sit by her bedside, spelling their exhausted, heartsick parents. One night Miranda woke, vomiting, from a drugged slumber. Unable to quell the spasms, even to catch her breath, she threw herself off the bed in agony and crouched trembling on the floor like an animal, horrid blasts of air and fluid shooting up her esophagus and out her anus, tears, sweat and spit spattering the carpet. She cried, over and over, "I'm dying, Barbie. I'm dying."

"She wanted me to leave. She was terrified. Her voice sounded like a little girl's. But it was all her own, the dying consumed her, she wanted to be alone. Her body was ripping itself apart, but she didn't want help or comfort. She wanted me to leave so I wouldn't distract her from the dying. She was tired of caring for people. What does that mean? I'm a doctor, but I don't know what it means. That year everyone abandoned me."

"The trouble with modern medicine," I tell her, "is that it has simply extended human life expectancy twenty or thirty years into the limbo of anticlimax — not something Neddy had to worry about, either."

We both flinch at the sound of Neddy's name, though we both also know that if I didn't just keep talking like this I'd have no recourse but to slash my wrists, eat rat poison, run a hose from my car exhaust or just beat my brains out with one of the whitewashed rocks lining the parking pad outside the cottage.

She says, "What modern medicine has taught me is that experience is suffering, and most of the time we have drugs for that."

Beyond the limestone ridge lies a tract of wild country called the Devil's Den. Bobcats haunt the tangled undergrowth, maybe a bear, plenty of deer, the motel owner tells me. The motel owner's name is Ben. He lives with his wife Marge, who hacks around the diminutive owner's suite with a tank of oxygen on a little cart and a mask over her face. Ben smokes in the breezeway by the neon sign that says OFFICE. He wears his long white hair pulled back in a ponytail so tight it seems to drag the skin of his bony face into a mask.

Ben and Marge have a son named Mike, who lives in exile in one of the guest cottages. Ben says Mike's a loner, which is short for a divorced part-time woodcutter who spends most of his time gambling at the harness track or riding around the Devil's Den on his four-wheel ATV, getting drunk. They also have a Brazilian grey monkey named Michael, which they keep caged in Mike's former bedroom in the owner's suite. Ben and Marge think this thin domestic joke is hilarious.

We are all accomplices, it seems. We will do almost anything, enact any cruelty, to keep from thinking about what we are not thinking about. And this strange antithesis of a romance which Dr. Tithonous and I prosecute in the little housekeeping cabin beneath the Devil's Den is nothing but a trick and a sign of what it is not. It would be a mistake to think that we are sad, precisely. It is closer to the truth to imagine Barbara, Annie and me (and Ben and Marge and Mike) pursuing our dark ecstasies with a certain rueful zest —

after all, we are not dead yet. Having watched Neddy slip out of the mist and then drift quietly back into the mist — always the mystery of the sweet half-smile — we lurch backward from the edge with a sharpened sense of self. The sounds Dr. Tithonous makes during sex are almost indescribable (as were the sounds her sister made grappling with her death). They haunt me still.

I tell you this mainly because it makes me feel better. It's not worth speaking otherwise. Language is eighty per cent consolation, twenty per cent aphrodisiac. Communication is an outmoded enterprise, honesty a fake, love a conservative political agenda. Sex is a form of prayer, a baroque topological assault upon the envelope of the soul. All the orifices are good because they get you closer to God. The only sense of self left to us is the sense of the self as actor, that is, when we are pretending to be someone else — hence our ruinous cult of Hollywood celebrity. It is as if we have all been inoculated with that same mysterious wasting sickness, contaminated with death.

One day when Barbara and I are in the throes of something or other, her beeper sounds. She shrugs her shirt and jeans over her pale, bruised body. Her lips are bleeding, her breasts are palimpsests of bruises fading from black to gold. She seems faintly noble, if not heroic, buttoning herself, tossing her long hair over her shoulders, staggering out past the shuttered windows into the blazing sunlight. Her lips wear a thin, rueful smile, the twin of Neddy's.

Left alone, I smoke a cigarette. But almost at once I fall prey to remembering, to my ineluctable past, to visions of empty nurseries, abandoned infant car seats, my wife's seeping breasts, her night cries, memories which inevitably drive me out in search of distraction. How can you sit alone after you've heard those words: "My baby is hungry. He needs to eat"?

Outside Mike is packing cans of beer into saddlebags in

preparation for his version of a nature hike, a jaunt through the Devil's Den on his ATV. I watch him in silence, but the silence only compels me to engage him in conversation, to make some claim on existence through the sound of my own voice.

I tell Mike this thing with Neddy has put me in a state. I ask him if he thinks Annie has the moral edge on me because she just sits in the nursery weeping, zonked on Zoloft and Restoril she gets from Dr. Tithonous. I tell him I can't stand to be with her, that I am scared to death of really feeling as bad as I feel, that she only reminds me of that. When I'm in that room with her, I say, I think I might have to kill her to get through this, kill her and then call in an air strike and nuke the nursery, the house, the yard (with that swing set I bought as kit and spent a weekend putting together), the whole damn city, and let loose a cloud of radiation that circumnavigates the globe, exterminating everything else.

Mike says, "Right."

He says very little at the best of times but generally knows exactly how to calm me down. I know he has his own family issues. Ben is always looking at Marge's breathing apparatus and saying things like, "Can't wait till we get that shit out of the house." And Marge has told me with some enthusiasm that Ben has an aneurysm, that he'll probably die the next time he sneezes. They both tell me they made a will giving the motel to the Brazilian grey monkey instead of Mike, though they made Mike the executor. They despise Mike for some obscure failure, some purely human thing, I suspect.

Mike himself traces it back to when he was six and his guinea pig Pinky died and he cried too much. He says Ben felt so bad that he couldn't fix things that he decided to blame Mike. "He decided I was a wimp and a crybaby," says Mike. "I've been a flop ever since."

I tell him it's a fundamental human trait to be inhuman to other humans. And then I say, "Maybe it's a kind of love, you know, not wanting to disrupt your father's view of things."

Mike says, "Right."

And then he says, "You want to go into the Den and raise Hell?"

And I say, "I'm in the mood to drive all the way to the bottom and kick Beelzebub in the nuts."

We climb past the deer lick where Mike puts out corn and salt through the winter, through a narrow gorge along an old logging road as far as a row of water-filled caves cut into the side of a hill, a former graphite mine abandoned at the turn of the last century. A cold wind blows steadily out of those caves. The soft rock above the gaping entries seems ready to fall at any moment. They could be the gates of Hell. Mike says a hunter disappeared into those caves once, going after a dog that fell through the ice early one spring.

We drink beer, sitting back to back against a young oak growing up from the top of a ridge of mine tailings.

"We're sitting on history," Mike says. I have never known him to wax philosophical, and I take it as a sign of advanced drunkenness. I myself can't stop thinking about our earlier conversation.

I say, "I don't think there is any such thing as love, or love is just humouring the other person, not wanting to disrupt her vision of things."

"Two people humouring each other?" Mike asks.

"No," I say. "I don't think it works like that. One or the other." And then I add, "I think people can't stand to be in love, that it makes them nervous, that they try to wreck it because the memory of love is everlasting whereas love itself is always fleeting. I read in the paper about this new condition called reactive attachment disorder, where people keep themselves in constant physical pain to ward off the larger emotional pain of the loss of love. Now no one said they were going to lose love, but they might. It's the terrible thought that love might end that pushes people to destroy love and themselves."

"That's probably what I've got," says Mike. "I had it before they invented it," he says.

He pulls a .357 handgun from his saddlebag, and we take turns potting the trees. I am a terrible shot, but Mike can nip the twigs off branches. We shoot and shoot, and when we run out of bullets, a litter of fresh-fallen twigs and leaves lies about us.

We pack up and head back down to the Royal. Mike fetches a fresh clip from his cabin, and, for no reason at all except that it seems like a good idea, we head over to the owner's suite. Ben is away. Marge is sleeping, snoring into her oxygen mask. We sneak into his old bedroom, where Michael, the Brazilian grey monkey, darts up at the sound of visitors. The sweet smell of pine chips and rotting fruit mixed with the acidic tang of monkey piss rises from the floor of his cage. A pennant from Niagara Falls, a KISS poster and a plastic dream-catcher, remnants of Mike's boyhood, adorn the otherwise Spartan walls. A plastic ME-109, built from a kit, swings on a length of fishing line. But there is no furniture, just the cage.

For some reason, I think the room is an image of the inside of my mind, or Mike's mind. I am almost too drunk to know which is which. Mike holds the pistol to Michael's head. The monkey, after his initial enthusiasm, has lapsed into apathetic torpor. He squats on the floor of the cage, flipping his flaccid, worm-like penis back and forth with the back of his hand. He peers at the gun without interest and then, as if understanding what's to come, places his other hand over his eyes, the long fingers seeming to stretch almost half-way around his head. His long, skinny limbs make him look insect-like, but the overall effect — the steel bars, the flapping penis, the awkward crouch — is of pathos, of things not in their right place, of interminable anxiety.

I feel a thrill of dread, an almost delicious anticipation of some terrible climax toward which the day or my whole life has been tending. The smell from the cage or the vision of monkey brains soaking into the pine chips makes me gag. But I cannot tear myself away. I am already worried that this will end too soon, that Mike and I will run out of interesting things to do for the rest of the afternoon. I am dying, Annie, I think. I am dying.

But then, as if the whole thing had been a whim, Mike lowers the barrel of the gun, feels with his fingertips above the door lintel for a key, unlocks the cage and grabs Michael by the scruff of his neck. One-handed, he slides open a window which looks out upon the trail to the Devil's Den. I can just see the deer lick two hundred yards into the woods and the limestone walls of the gorge poking out of the pines. Mike kicks the screen out of the window and heaves the monkey into the yard. Michael falls in a dusty heap, then resumes his apathetic squat.

But it is cold out there, the chill wind (it seems to come down from those caves, seems to be following us) ruffles his fur. The monkey peers about, then squints at us watching him from the window. You can see questions beginning to form, warring with years of habit, boredom and loneliness. He dabs at the dry pine needles with his fingertips, watches a handful fly away in the breeze. He faces the wind coming over the Devil's Den, and suddenly the shadows within his eyes deepen as if opening into a long-locked room.

The wind in his fur gives him an ancient warrior look. (What this really means I don't know. And I was drunk. Perhaps all meaning is context, or perhaps I was simply prey to sentiments which no longer had a natural outlet after Neddy's death, but I saw him so.) Mike's reaction is to drop to his knees, cradle his shooting arm against the window sill and take aim. A ball of terror collects in my stomach.

Mike aims, fires. But the bullet flies wide. The monkey's head snaps around, his suspicious eyes absorbing the picture of the two men and the gun, none of which he understands. But some intuition, some reserve of instinct warns him — the air seems suddenly to thicken around us. And he begins an easy four-legged lope up the hillside.

Mike blasts away till his clip is empty. His face glows crimson above his collar, his gun-hand trembles crazily as though some invisible being were struggling to wrest the gun away from him. He looks beaten, defeated, or like a man about to have a stroke. He shouldn't have missed. I wonder why he did. The monkey pauses at the deer lick, squats again, cranes his neck to look first up the trail and then back at us. He is clearly uncertain about the future, about bobcats and the cold. But uncertainty holds him only a moment, and he bravely resumes his upward journey in the direction of who knows what bloody future hurtling toward him.

"He'll be dead in a week," says Mike, breathing heavily, watching the wispy grey fur of the monkey's back disappear into the trees. "If the cats don't get him, he'll starve to death."

Mike starts to laugh, starts, then pauses to see what it feels like to laugh at this juncture, then continues, the volume rising in waves. I can't tell if this is an act or not. Perhaps the whole thing has been an act. Or perhaps there are good reasons for Marge and Ben to keep their son in one of the farther cottages. His face looks like the head of a match bursting into flame.

I can only think how heroic the monkey looks in contrast to his human brother, how satisfying a prospect his night of freedom and violent death seems. And I ponder the mystery of that judgment. This is the old romantic trap, I think. In what sense can it be true that the monkey's brief, sweet sojourn in the Den can be more real, more authentic, than a life in a warm cage?

I am sick in bed for three days after this bout of drunkenness (what my father used to call a toot), but it wakes me up, wakes up my moral being. I once thought you could get through anything by striking attitudes and spouting a little philosophy. But that's not true. I am not going to get through this, and what I am doing with Dr. Tithonous is wrong. I mean I am going to get through it. I am alive, after all. But my life has changed irrevocably. The person I am now and the person I was before Neddy died are discontinuous, though related, like second cousins once removed.

On top of everything else, I decide my marriage is coming apart. Little indications of seismic upheaval abound: the way Annie drifts out of rooms as I enter, the sound of uncontrollable sobbing behind locked doors, her perfect composure when she finally does appear, her sudden interest in therapy and her reconnection with an old girlfriend named Rosellen who recently moved back to town. There is nothing definite, only an incremental decline, a mysterious wasting.

Annie knows nothing of my affair with Dr. Tithonous, but she accuses me with her eyes when she thinks I am not looking. These silent accusations are troubling in their implication. What betrayal am I being charged with? Did I wish Neddy dead? Am I taking it all too lightly with my endless golf-playing? What can she think? To me, her anger seems gratuitous, its own species of betrayal. Does she think I actually want to act the way I am acting, that I have any control? I stopped getting what I wanted the moment Neddy died. Everything since then can only be described as fate or gesture. Am I really to be blamed because I am no less capable than she of bridging the silence between us?

Not that there weren't signs of trouble before Neddy was born. Annie and I were both ambivalent, but we were both also tired of our dithering. So we went ahead and made the baby, and briefly the act of taking a risk restored to us our sense of adventure, brought us together as nothing had since the very beginning of our relationship, when, likewise impelled by panache and a willingness to gamble, we threw ourselves together. Character is action, action is fate. You are someone when you do something. The rest of the time you wallow. Life becomes this endless tension between wallowing and little abortive attempts to compose a self through action. The polar modes of existence: wallowing and a desperate, mindless darting. Annie and I are just two normal, modern people caught in the soup — but she blames me for this.

Annie and I met one summer between college terms in a little café around the corner from the Rodin Museum in Paris. I was travelling alone. She was with her brother and his fiancée, a buxom Californian who resented having to drag Annie along wherever they went. I had watched them wander through the museum. The brother and his fiancée were clearly bored — they kissed in front of

The Kiss, they held hands in front of the hands, they leaned on each other in front of *The Burghers of Calais*. Annie looked forlorn, miserable, her face pale, as though she hadn't slept. You actually had to look twice to see her beauty.

I followed them to the café, then made myself a nuisance, asking directions, folding my map out onto their table. I asked Annie to come with me for the afternoon. She said no. The fiancée urged her to have an adventure. You could see relief flooding all three faces. "You saved me from my version of a wicked stepmother," she said afterward, laughing. But, equally, she had saved me from a terrible loneliness and self-perpetuating insecurity. And her laughter had a forced quality, as if she were trying to put the best face on things.

How this sense of uneasy relief and gratitude turned into love is a caution and a mystery. Perhaps it was only that we did not know what love was and mistook whatever it was we were feeling for love. Or that, both of us being unable to bear disappointment in the other, we manufactured an enthusiasm that was otherwise lacking in order to feast on the delight in the other's eyes. Hence the eerie emptiness, the silence which seemed always to surround our love, the sense that if we did not keep upping the ante, risking more, our love would disappear. This, it seems to me, is the essence of romantic love, love founded upon its own impossibility, love which paradoxically feeds upon itself in order to grow. In time, Annie and I both grew to feel left out of our marriage. Who were those two people fornicating so energetically, so joylessly, upon the counterpane? Not she, not I. Would Neddy have made us real again?

My new moral self, discovered after bottoming out and conspiring to murder a Brazilian grey monkey at the Royal Motel, decides to make a clean breast of things. Perhaps this is not a new moral self, perhaps it is only the old pathological self that just has to keep stirring things up in order to feel alive. It's difficult to tell. I meet Dr. Tithonous at the Royal and tell her I can't see her anymore. She tells me she isn't wearing any underwear, that there is dampness trickling down the insides of her thighs, that she has longed for this moment, the moment of rejection. Weeping, she falls to her knees and, fumbling with my belt, begs me desperately to make love to her, a locution she has never used in the past. She has become a glutton for humiliation. Why do I feel, once again, that we are acting out some universal drama? Our obsession with one another is about to transform itself into shame and loathing on her side and mild distaste and irritation on mine. A week ago we were at each other like dogs in heat, and a week from now we'll both be wishing it had never happened. It's a wonder to me that the so-called experts haven't realized that we're all going around in a state of chronic low-grade schizophrenia, that identity is a fiction.

My new moral self drives home with a certain self-righteous precision and discovers Annie in the nursery, rocking almost imperceptibly in the little rocking chair she meant to use for nursing Neddy, listening to the panda bear mobile playing "Twinkle, twinkle, little star." She's in there communing with our son, I think. But then again maybe she is in there communing with me — for this is now my favourite room in the house, the place where I spend my lonely hours. I smell of sex with Dr. Tithonous (my new moral self winces at this admission). Annie looks sad, pensive and suddenly more beautiful than I have ever seen her, as if after all the undignified suffering she has achieved some deeper knowledge of the meaning of things.

I had marched into the house full of hatred for myself and my wife, ready to slay her with my revelations, ready to demolish her with honesty for all that pathetic flailing about I hate in myself (so much for the new moral self — whenever you feel the moral self waking within, you can bet an act of injustice and inhumanity is about to follow). But she only glances up at me with a bemused, slightly embarrassed smile on her face which reminds me of nothing so much as Neddy, oh, these eons ago. For it was her smile I was seeing on his face, only I'd forgotten.

And all at once I feel a welling up of love for Annie, love and passion and desire. My limbs tremble as contrary emotions surge through me. My eyes grow hot, heavy-lidded with tears. I remember the splendour of making Neddy. I recall the terrible hope in our hearts. I want just to touch her and go on touching her for the rest of my life, to catch her hand and put my cheek against hers so that I might feel the warmth of her flesh and smell the sweetness of her breath as it goes in and out and remember, oh, remember what hope was like. There has never been anything else I ever wanted and nothing more I will ever want. I am completely undone, unstrung, helpless.

She says, "Hey, you." She touches my foot with hers and holds up her arms to pull me in. Her eyes are full of mischief, a weary merriment, irresistible eyes.

I hesitate because now I have a terrible truth to tell, something unforgivable that will come slamming down on us like a steel door, crushing this sudden afflatus of love.

I call it love, for want of a better word — I don't know what it is, really. Beyond us there is a void, and inside us there is a void. At the centre, the self is inscrutable. We ride the dark, lunar surfaces of unknown objects our whole lives long; we are receivers of messages the provenance of which is as obscure as death itself. It seems to test us, to drown us, grow us, betray us, destroy us. Before it, we are alone. And yet between this void and the shallow dogmas of psycho-therapeutics there remains some residue, some faint sediment of — what? The thing you can't see for looking at it, the thing disappearing at the corner of your eye, the thing not conceived in any of your philosophies, the thing that is not the void and not the half-crazy, shambling beast of desire that dogs our lives (what the Buddhists call "the little self"). This is the place where love resides, if love resides.

I lay my head upon her lap. The rocking chair is still. Annie strokes my temples, the nape of my neck, and, sobbing because my heart is broken, I tell her that our boy is dead, that this is the only real thing that's happened, that getting so close to reality is like putting your head in a giant wall socket, that every certainty has been upended, the linchpin knocked out of my life, the keystone dropped from the arch. I can't figure out how to take another step, but I wander on, embarrassed by my own seeming indestructibility. I can't say who is telling my feet to move. It's not me giving the orders. "I tried so hard," I sob. I don't know why my heart seems suddenly to break again when I say the words. "I tried so hard." But the tears are gushing out of me, my body is wracked with sadness.

The rhythm of Annie's caresses never falters. She says nothing. I feel the gentle insistence of the flesh of her thigh against my cheek, reminding me of her sexual presence, of our consequential passions. I think how my present prostration is the only correct response to the world, that if we could see the world the way it really is, there would be nothing but this weeping and biting of hands. I think, now I am where I belong.

But presently, without looking into her face, I begin to tell Annie about my afternoons at the Royal Motel with Dr. Tithonous. (How many times, in the grip of some outré perversity, did I recall the vision of the doctor crouched beside the bed, whispering into Annie's ear, the soiled nightgown, the streaming breasts, both women mysteriously out of themselves, forgetful of me? How many times did I pity the doctor for her subterranean hungers? It seemed, yes, that she was the most tragic of us all, the one to whom science had revealed all secrets but who had drifted farthest from the truth. What is the truth? Once I told her, "Modern medicine is a crutch we should throw away." Impossible to know what I meant.)

I can barely get the words out, but each sound I utter increases my confidence in the story. Somehow, I suppose, I'd thought language would prove incapable of conveying the monstrous details, that I wouldn't be able to tell her. But the very miracle of turning my assignations into sentences and paragraphs has the odd effect of domesticating them, making them feel reasonable, part of the known world (another function of language: it renders everything it touches trivial and slightly seedy). I hadn't gone beyond the moon — I had met our doctor at a motel because I was upset about what happened to Neddy, who died at three months of a mysterious wasting disease. This sounds so plausible, and Annie's response — silence — seems so benign that I almost stop feeling guilty, though moments later my heart races with anxiety over the obvious discrepancies between my words and the facts, language's inadequacy as a device for communicating, signalled here by Annie's first words when she does begin to speak — something about a monkey, as if I have somehow mixed up the story about the monkey with the story about Dr. Tithonous.

Fresh reasons for despair — I can't even confess to my wife without inspiring a misunderstanding, without the words somehow being misconstrued. The thing is absolutely impossible — she can't see into my heart. Or have I simply been lying again without knowing it? I repeat here that the only real thing that's happened is that Neddy died. All the rest — Annie crying, "My baby's hungry, I have to feed my baby," my affair with Dr. Tithonous, the attempted murder of the monkey — all the rest is true, too, but in the manner of a code or a substitute for the real thing. The sad truth is that part of me already no longer believes Neddy lived and died. The New Agers call this the healing process. Mourning has its rhythms and stages, and pretty soon it is as if the thing itself didn't happen, just the mourning and the healing. The aftermath becomes the thing — like the intergalactic radiation that remains our only evidence for the Big Bang at the beginning of Time. By substitution, by the metaphoric process of language, we move incrementally away from the edge of reality, back into the everyday zone of safety and lies — we ought to put a stop to healing, I think.

Annie gently asks again about the monkey. This time I have to look at her face to see if indeed she might not have gone completely insane (always a distinct possibility with human beings), but there is only that curious smile, Neddy's smile, about which now I see I was mistaken. It's not uncertain, wan and etiolate, as I had thought. Rather it is a smile of affection, only slightly uncertain of response, waiting for a response. It occurs to me suddenly, blindingly, that Neddy loved us — that was the message of the smile — and that he knew he was loved.

This realization unleashes fresh grief. I am a boy again, sobbing inconsolably over the unfairness of life. I have never felt such pain and, simultaneously, such release — an access of fatigue and self-pity. Annie cradles my face against her breasts and begins to rock again ever so slightly.

All at once I am kissing her, struggling to undo the buttons of her shirt. She releases me slightly from our embrace to help. Her breasts are large, slightly under-inflated, as it were, as they begin to shrink to their normal size. Flawed like this, they have never seemed more desirable. They tell me a story, something about the life of women. I suck them, tasting the bittersweet taste of her milk. She rocks me, croons one of those children's songs she had been memorizing through her pregnancy. And soon we are making love on the floor, very carefully, very tenderly, without thinking about birth control, just the way we did when we made Neddy.

It is a strange sort of excitement, full of history and sadness, calm somehow, without the usual agitation of sexual desire. We look into each other's eyes and feel our bodies rising, but we are distant from that. The thing that is empty inside me is pouring itself into Annie and into the minatory and morbid future.

Nothing makes sense. And it has stopped being a story. I have to fight to keep my anxiety for sense and explanations from corrupting the moment. The moment is already corrupt when I think that it doesn't make sense, for there is no perception without words. And there is no such thing as the things we call by the words "love" and "human being" and "soul." I can only hope that, by some backwards logic, the moment that makes no sense somehow makes the most sense, that the truth is true because it is unrecognizable. In this moment, I also do not recognize myself or my wife. But I feel a surge of forgiveness and generosity flowing from her, out of the mysterious and alien emptiness that is all I can know of her. It has none of the conventional passion or even coziness of the thing we normally call love. All that has burned off with the loss of Neddy.

As we come back to ourselves, we are like tired, wounded soldiers, strangers to one another, supporting each other out of the battle. We cannot save each other, we cannot escape, but there is some human dignity to be claimed in the comradeship of the doomed. We hold each other, a little abashed at what we have done. And I can see the old pieties and anxieties beginning to reassert themselves in Annie's eyes. There is some hurt there now, the beginnings of resentment (the feeling of the age), though I can also see that she is fighting this, clearly surprised and proud of her spiritual daring.

I myself am startled by a sudden perception of Annie's mysterious depths, how different she is from any expectation I have of her, how she is herself, astonishing and other. I cannot calculate the reasons for this, but where I could only think to touch her with my anger and violence, she has found a way to reach back with love and forgiveness. This gesture is transformative just as it is tentative and temporary. So much of what is good in life has this quality of fleetingness, a glimpse snatched through a closing door, an infant dying. But it makes me love her back, though I don't know what it means to say that.

Six months later they find Ben and Marge dead together in the bedroom, holding hands. There is a note that says they decided they could not live without each other and were afraid they would soon lose the chance to make that choice themselves. Suddenly Mike owns the Royal Motel. He stops drinking out of shock, not because his parents killed themselves but because of that note. "I thought they hated each other," he says. He thought they hated him, too, and now his whole universe has been turned upside down.

I myself am puzzled by the violent shifting of things, the lack of continuity between words and actions. Nothing in the way they presented themselves had prepared me for the couple's dramatic liebestod. I say, "Mike, sometimes it seems as if life is designed specifically to demolish every certainty, every categorical statement. Or else it's a novel being written by an inattentive author who cannot even bother to keep the characters straight."

Since that fateful afternoon, there has been no sign of the Brazilian grey monkey — no body, no telltale fur patches or crushed, half-eaten bones. It is as if he walked into the Devil's Den and vanished. Mike, who has had a complete change of heart about the monkey and searches for him constantly (leaving little caches of food among the rocks), believes the monkey just kept walking and somehow is on his way back to Brazil, home.

Iglaf and Swan

THIS IS HOW IT GOES: a boy named Iglaf, whose parents had immigrated from Estonia in the 1940s after much trouble in their native land, met a girl named Swan at a potluck supper and open mike poetry reading in the basement of the Estonian Church on Broadview the summer of 1969. They became lovers that night, burnt a hole in his mattress with an overturned candle, drank wine from peanut butter jars and read their poems aloud between embraces. Near dawn they fell asleep in each other's arms, but then Swan woke up, wrapped a sheet around her breasts, sniffed the smell of burnt ticking in her hair, and stared at him. What was she trying to make out? What had disturbed her sleep?

The fierceness of her regard woke Iglaf from a dream — as he remembered it later, something about a book he had read or written. He rubbed his eyes, then met her gaze. Something in her face turned his heart to stone. He knew that he loved her. He knew that she loved him. But he knew Swan would never stay. His life was over in that moment. All hope abandoned. The future a nightmare of cajolery, recrimination, begging and jealousy. In that moment, he knew he would lose himself trying to keep her, and, having made that sacrifice, fail. But also in that moment he decided that a year, a month, even a day of Swan's love was worth any sacrifice. He even convinced himself that his was a romantic gesture, that there was some glory in a life of misery, some salvation in throwing himself away for those breasts, those eyes. In any case, it was already too late, and he knew it. And later it occurred to him that maybe he had never really had the courage to be himself, a poet, an adventurer, anyway, that he had needed a way out of that terrible struggle, that he found the lesser vision comfortably definite.

Swan, an insightful and intelligent girl, comprehended all this in an instant. The light of love guttered in her heart, a flash of loathing exploded in her head, though she was careful to disguise it with a rueful smile and a knowing twinkle in her eye. Iglaf interpreted this knowing twinkle as the kindling of desire for him. With a rush of gratitude, he took her in his arms, and they began to make love again, slowly, despairingly. She wept this time. It hurt when he moved inside her, though she whispered "I love you" over and over as his passion rose. When it was over, she loathed herself as well.

It took Iglaf and Swan ten years to separate. He was teaching high school English in Forest Hills, she spent mornings looking after their daughter Lily and afternoons working at a futon store on St. Clair, where she made love to the owner in a dusty storage room. The owner's name was Kreuzen. He was her father's age, a Czech émigré, also bitter, lost. He made love violently, briskly, without any preamble or pretence of emotion. His face was a rigid mask of anger when he came. He would tell her nothing about his past. The mask was all she had. But this suited Swan. Kreuzen's wife had left him years before. He had a grown son about Swan's age, who, once a month, would stand at the shop door, shouting, "You fucking pig! You fucking pig!" "He's an actor," said Kreuzen. "He can't get work. You have to hate your father if you're an actor and can't work."

Kreuzen would sit in the storeroom behind the futon shop for hours during the day or talk in his own language to a steady stream of shabby visitors. Swan would read him her poetry, to which he would respond with a tired shrug. Sometimes she would meet one or another of the Czech men who came to visit Kreuzen. Each time she would tell Iglaf, and the brief spasms of emotion which followed seemed to sustain them, feed their love.

Iglaf put on weight, wore vests and threadbare second-hand tweed jackets, smoked a pipe and affected a world-weary wisdom which he used to seduce a series of female students. These affairs followed a hair-raising pattern of infatuation, obsession and then disengagement which involved public scenes, hysterical tears on the girl's part, bitter recrimination. Twice he nearly got fired from his job, but each time Swan saved him by sitting through the internal inquiries holding his hand (the first time she actually breastfed Lily during the proceedings), facing down angry parents, testifying about his goodness, his professionalism, the wonder of their marriage. Always, Iglaf managed to shift the blame onto the girl. But, without saying anything, Iglaf and Swan both knew they wouldn't be able to save him a third time.

One summer in the late seventies, Swan enrolled in an evening writing course. She did this because, she told herself, some outside structure — a regular class, an instructor — would get her writing poetry again. "I lost myself in my marriage," she told Iglaf, who said nothing, but winced. It was a subtle gesture he had perfected over the years, a slight lowering of the shoulders, a shadowing of the eyes, a turning away. Swan and Lily reacted to the wince with guilt, a stab of pain. Swan would rage inwardly about the wince, but Lily spent her days trying to keep her father from wincing. She thought that when he didn't wince it was love.

Of them all, Kreuzen was the most truthful. He said, "You never stopped writing poetry. You're just not very good at it. You're like my son. You use art and your lives as excuses for each other." Swan spent the afternoon weeping on Kreuzen's cot, then dragged all her

notebooks, drafts, diaries — everything she kept at the futon shop
— to the dumpster. She knew she was finished, that she had failed
at her whole life. But oddly that realization made her feel cleaned
out and powerful. Kreuzen watched dispassionately. He said, "Now
you'll leave us. You're making a dramatic exit. I've done my job."
When she tried to kiss him, he told her to get out.

A week later she was sleeping with her writing teacher and
trying not to remember what Kreuzen had said, that she had ever
been in the back of the futon store. The writing instructor had
published one book of poems years before and showed no promise
any longer of writing another. He was married but made a practice
of sleeping with at least one of his students each term, in fact had
come to think of this as one of the requirements of his profession. At
first he had seen his student lovers as the bright new stars who
would rouse him from his artistic slumber. He had believed himself
in love — several times. But now he resented Swan for her naive
hopes, her sentimental and self-serving little poems and her lovely
body. Rather than giving him new energy, she seemed almost to be
sucking the energy out of him, though he could not fathom how.
Everything he did he did out of anger.

Swan, for her part, saw him as a great soul — she mistook his
fatigued restraint for a species of spiritual tranquility. She called
him her poetry guru and was, briefly, cheerful and optimistic.
While she was sleeping with the poetry teacher, she was also beginning to hope she might rebuild her marriage. Her new sexual energy
radiated throughout the house. Even Lily noticed, and the little girl
began to imitate her mother's hip-rolling walk, her casual way of
strolling through rooms half-clothed, her habit of singing to herself
the current pop tunes that were already a little too young for her.

Iglaf noticed, too, and took advantage of the new warmth. Their
sex had never been better: nights they smoked dope and experi-
mented with each other's bodies, fantasizing together, playing
roles, pushing each other to new ecstasies. But this new sex was also
strangely empty, and one day Lily woke up and caught her parents

in bed with another woman, one of Swan's poetry friends, a pretty blond girl with a tattoo on her belly and a knowing eye.

A year later, Swan and her tattooed friend were hitchhiking through Europe and North Africa. She had borrowed money from Iglaf and Kreuzen. Swan already felt too old for this, spent her days in a confusion of anxiety, moodiness and self-reproach until she found a new boy to fuck. She wrote long, witty, self-ironic letters to Lily and Kreuzen — sometimes the same letter to both — describing her tour as a series of comic-erotic misadventures. The letters made her feel creative again. They were easier to write than poetry. She ended each with a request for Kreuzen or Lily to keep the letter safe for the book she was going to make out of them when she came home.

Lily stayed with Iglaf. At first, after her parents separated, there had been an attempt to share custody. They had shuttled her back and forth between them in taxis with a little duffel full of clothes, stuffed toys and homework. They had argued endlessly over child support, clothing allowances, gym fees, drop-off times, sick days. Swan had brought home lovers. Lily could hear them making love in the bedroom from the daybed where she slept. Iglaf had grown weepy, depressed. He blamed himself for everything, especially blamed himself for falling in love with Swan and wasting his talent. Lily tried to comfort him. She kept his apartment clean, did the washing, cooked small meals or ordered out. Iglaf watched television while Lily bustled around, trying to be cheerful. Years later, he would say he had had a nervous breakdown.

Now, Lily was ten. She hid her mother's letters from Iglaf. He had gone cold to her, rarely spoke, dressed with elaborate punctilio for work and wore a series of flamboyant hats to cover his thinning hair. Everything he said and did around Lily was a rebuke, as if to say, "All this is because of you." He talked to women on the phone long into the night, his voice dropping to a stage whisper, then bursting into loud peals of laughter. He bought pornographic magazines by mail and took to sunbathing naked in a hidden corner up on the roof of their building. But he never saw anyone, never went out. He would sit in front of the TV with an unread mystery novel in his lap and a can a beer in his hand, spend hours like that.

Once, Lily overheard Iglaf telling one of his telephone women that he was writing again, that he had gotten through mourning his marriage and had found his voice. She was briefly hopeful. He had always said writing was the only thing that made him happy. But then she realized it was just a story he was telling, that all his art went into those late night phone conversations. What she remembered most from that period were Iglaf's maniacal smile, his lips stretched taut over his gums, his teeth shining big and too white against the tan of his face, and the heavy sag of his genitals in the bikini briefs he wore when he came slipping back from his tanning sessions.

Lily began to write, first poems, then stories, sweet little girl stories full of elves and fairies and made up words. She had a fantasy, a vision of her own death, and her father coming upon her writings in an old trunk under her bed, weeping at the beauty of her words. Pale, dressed in black, she roamed the city, nervous, fearful, always looking down but conscious of the way lone men and boys stared at her, vaguely excited by this. On her eleventh birthday, she got a letter from her mother — the first in a month — with an amusing account of how Swan had caught herpes from a man she met in a Venice disco.

Swan was still sick when she came back from Europe. She had stopped eating, grown gaunt. Her breath was bad, her sores refused to clear up. She imagined she had cancer. She told Lily, "I'm scared. I can't stop myself from doing anything but eat." At first, because she had no money and nowhere to go, she stayed with Iglaf, sleeping on a cot in Lily's room. She slept through the mornings, went to yoga classes, drank herbal remedies she bought from a Chinese apothecary off Spadina Avenue. In the night she would dream the same dream over and over: she was on a stage under a fierce spotlight, naked. The audience, men and women, jeered and pelted her with garbage. She would begin to touch herself, almost fainting from the shame and dark excitement, while the shouts and laughter grew louder and louder. And in her sleep, she would roll over on her belly and begin to masturbate, sometimes waking Lily with her sighs, waking herself when she came, hating herself.

Iglaf was thirty-three, looked years older with his thinning hair, sun-hardened skin and salt-and-pepper beard. He frightened Lily and Swan with his manic cheerfulness, his too-wide smile that seemed to conceal a violent threat. He would play the gracious host around Swan, then lose control of himself and try to paw her, begging her to make love. Once Lily woke up to find her father naked in her bedroom, sobbing noisily, trying to pull the blankets off Swan, Swan's sleepy, petulant voice whispering, "No, no, no." This frigid, hysterical travesty of a family mystified Lily. She thought the forced cheerfulness of her parents, seated across from each other at the dinner table, was love, but love made her feel as if there were an iron belt around her belly, cinched tighter and tighter each day. Love made her want to die.

She had a boyfriend now, a pale, skinny kid who called himself Captain Nemo, which he said was the Latin word for nobody. He was four years older than Lily, but somehow naive and unworldly, which appealed to her. He wore his hair in a pink Mohawk and carved up his hands and arms with ballpoint pen tattoos. They would wander the city together, day and night, Nemo declaiming his rebellious philosophy of life in hoarse, fearful whispers while Lily listened, barely uttering a word. They would go into the ravines to smoke dope when Lily had money or sometimes sniff glue when she didn't. They drank cheap wine once and vomited over each other. Sometimes they would try to make love, but they were nervous and inexperienced and had no notion of tenderness. Nemo mostly came before he could enter her. Lily hated sex, but she was deeply attached to Nemo, would do anything for him.

It was a strange, narrow world Lily had entered. She cut school, had no friends besides Nemo. She had been betrayed in so many ways that she could not imagine a world of constancy and trust. As she closed herself off more and more from the outside just to keep safe, she even began to feel that she had betrayed herself. Her confusion and loathing turned inward. She seemed to walk among the dead. Even Nemo noticed how quiet she had become, how she seemed to soak up words and energy without reacting, how every-thing sank into Lily, seemed to tremble on the surface a moment, and then eerily slip out of sight. Her deadness frightened him.

Lily was still writing. She no longer knew why. She filled note-book after notebook with rambling fantasy romances, tales of gentle knights in armour and princesses under spells or trapped in towers, goblins, ogres, dwarves, elves and sorcerers. When she wrote, she remembered her father's agonized attempts to drive himself at his desk or her mother's voice mumbling poems to herself while Lily drifted off to sleep in her crib — her very own Madonna of the Poems. She remembered all her parents' brave dreams and their disappointments. She was in love with the sad drama of their lives. But when Captain Nemo finally blushed and stuttered out the words "I love you," she fled from him as if wounded.

This is a dark story, growing darker still: before she turned fifteen, Lily was dead. At the end, she had come to think of herself as a mistake, a misprint, an unintended result. It seemed a simple thing to fix with Valium from Swan's medicine cabinet and a plastic garbage bag from under the sink. Lily had learned to adore unconsciousness, blackouts and altered states — ecstasy was in becoming nothing. Nothingness had a voluptuousness she found nowhere else in life. She became greedy for it the way others become greedy for sex. Nemo noticed when no one else did. He noticed the way her eyes worked, the way she stopped looking at him and, instead, stared greedily and nervously at the drugs he brought. Unconsciousness became her companion. Nothingness became her lover. It wiped out her childish fantasies, which she had come to despise. She stopped writing when she knew no one would ever read what she wrote.

Briefly, on the night of Lily's death, Iglaf and Swan were together again. Swan was incoherent, bereft; Iglaf put his heart into arranging things for Lily and thought about nothing else. His grief and his quiet competence gave Iglaf a dignity Swan had never noticed before. To Iglaf, his woundedness was a sign that had no meaning until his daughter died, and when she died, he was suddenly whole. Her death gave him a role he had been practicing for all his life. But the way he bore his suffering comforted Swan. They had lost everything; no one else knew how much, and how much they had subconsciously depended on Lily to make up their losses, to be their audience and interlocutor. Now Swan wanted his dignity to be a model for her own. When Iglaf dropped Swan at her apartment, she asked him to stay.

At first, he only held her; she brewed tea; they reminded each other of the night Lily was born and made each other weep. Momentarily, Iglaf lost his composure; in Swan's arms, he moaned, "What have we done?" and she said, "Shh, my darling" and kissed him. They both knew there was some trickery involved; they had acted so long, they no longer yearned for an end to the acting but for clear and simple parts, as close as most of us come to honesty. Swan lit candles and read Lily's poems aloud, while Iglaf slouched in her bedroom easy chair, his waistcoat unbuttoned, his arms hanging down, looking like a Victorian illustration. When they made love, finally, they wept and said Lily's name. They had never before felt so close, and the closeness aroused them. Without saying anything, they both knew they wanted to make another child, to call back the girl who had died, the family they had never been. They made love that way, as though they were in love, their soft, pathetic voices whispering to each other desperately of love and promises.

For a moment, they both forgot they had other lovers, that their lives had become petty, shallow and tawdry. Iglaf poured himself into Swan again and again with an abandonment he had never felt. He caught himself gloating over his prowess but pushed the thought from his mind. Swan submitted — to everything. She had never been so open to a man, but, thinking that, comparing this moment to others, she felt the edge of self-consciousness rising and pictured Lily's body to drive her back into the ecstasy of loss. With Lily gone, they both thought, there is no one else and no tomorrow. They only wished that the moment could go on and on, that they could exist forever on the cusp of someone else's death, that they could always feel this important, tragic and redeemed.

The next day, they lingered in bed as long as they could, alternating fits of weeping with laughter and a kind of childish, gleeful lust. But they were exhausted, and the pure orgasms of the night before escaped them. A different kind of sadness grew in them, a sense of emptiness and failure, as Iglaf made the necessary phone calls, trying moment by moment to keep the world at bay. Swan made breakfast; they looked at photo albums and read the poems again. Then Iglaf left to get changed, and Swan's latest boyfriend came by to comfort her. But through the funeral and the wake, they had a kind of intensity together. And they both knew they would never feel this close to love again.

Soon Swan was living with a painter on Beverley Street, a man with a loft in the old clothing district on Spadina for a studio, a gruff, silent man who painted lucrative, if old-fashioned, abstract expressionist works on large canvasses for corporate clients and loathed himself. Swan realized she fell for men who hated themselves and hated her and called it love. She had figured this out from her therapist, who also hated himself and had seduced her. She did not think the therapist was either wise or a guru. Sex had become a plumbing issue for Swan. When she watched her painter, she wondered what he thought, painstakingly but mechanically applying the colour. She thought how hopeless it all must seem. "It's not about hope," he said. "I get paid to be a cliché, which is better than being a cliché and not getting paid for it."

Iglaf was in therapy, too, trying to fix himself, rid himself of the self-pity that dogged his life. He was living with a plain, depressed woman he called Rubenesque but whom he was not so secretly ashamed of. "She does things for him in bed no one else will," said Swan who had lost the anxious restraint that had once attracted men and become, suddenly, crude. Iglaf told everyone how his marriage had destroyed his writing and how no one in Canada could write anyway because it was a debased and barren culture. He invoked Lily and the names of other poetic suicides and somehow managed to imply that he was one of them, only not quite dead yet. He was always saying, "We must get together and talk about writing." He founded writers' groups at the school where he taught, groups mostly for serious girls and introverted boys. He loved to inspire in others the dream of his own noble failure, the mountains he had barely failed to climb, and a sense of their own mediocrity and doom within the context of Canada. He loved making the children feel bad about themselves while, on the surface, appearing to nurture them.

Swan herself was making a small splash in the Toronto poetry world as Lily's mother, as the guardian of her words. Swan carefully collected, organized and rewrote Lily's poems and diaries. It did not seem to bother her that the poems and diaries damned her, and, of course, she cut the most direct references, telling herself that occasionally Lily's thinking had been reductive and maladroit (we all blame our mothers and fathers). It seemed to Swan that Lily had been born sad, that she had been doomed from the beginning, and she presented herself as heroic and self-sacrificing in the face of her daughter's depression. Lily's poems came out, first in small magazines, then as a book. The critics compared her with Sylvia Plath and Anne Sexton and the boy poet Chatterton. And when she read them in public, Swan briefly forgot that they weren't her poems. She felt like herself, beautiful and poetic, the centre of attention, with the lights shining down and her strong, unfaltering voice declaiming the words of the one person she had truly loved (who, in those moments, did not seem distinguishable from herself).

For Iglaf, who once or twice came to Swan's readings, these moments spawned a strange dementia. He saw himself and Swan reading their poetry nearly twenty years before in the church basement on Broadview, remembered making love, the smell of burnt ticking, the sultry resonance of Swan's voice and the long, shameful years that followed, and making love again the night Lily died. He remembered Lily, though he could not remember her well, just as he could no longer remember who he was himself. That he was partly aware of this only made matters worse. As a test, he tried to remember the last poem he had read and loved. He shuddered. Paradoxically, he found a certain erotic pleasure in his shame, in submitting to the deep humiliation of each new moment. He tried to remember what Lily looked like. He tried to concentrate on the poems Swan was reading, but couldn't. His face wore that toothy grin, tears splashed down his cheeks. His eyes were fixed on Swan, but he saw nothing. He knew that it was all an act, that all he had was his shame, and that, even so, everything that had happened had happened for love.

. . .

All the rest is twilight, bits of life manufactured without hope. Iglaf and Swan are not old; there are no dramatic exits available. Swan marries the painter. She learns to cook and mounts elegant dinner parties at which she drinks too much and talks too loudly. She has a shrewd eye for human foible and makes an art of insidious seating arrangements. She loves to revive old feuds, or encourage lushes to backslide, or provoke jealous arguments between young lovers. Swan herself grows nervous and rancorous as these evenings wear on and often ends up being ushered to bed in tears before the party is over. She gets away with this because the painter is powerful and despises everyone and enjoys watching his wife make a fool of herself and his friends.

Iglaf marries the Rubenesque woman, who promptly becomes obese. He drags her around, embarrassment incarnate, though secretly his voluptuary tastes run to masochism, and she suits his darker fantasies. The Rubenesque woman, whipsawed between Iglaf's desires and his coldness, grows ever more depressed, tearful and needy. He adores young women, the younger the better, but, paradoxically, is quite safe now because he is so obvious and repulsive. He still corners earnest girls after class and exclaims, through that toothy grin, "We must talk about writing." Perversely, he seems to enjoy the discomfort he causes. For Iglaf, affection is corruption, and any effect is better than no effect.

From time to time, Swan and Iglaf meet, for they both still haunt the fringes of the Toronto literary scene. They cannot conceal their envy of youth and passion and, of course, writers who manage to write. They are fading, but desire never ends — only, after a time, it twists into some reduced caricature of itself. Iglaf and Swan have become the kind of readers who confuse criticism with discrimination.

But the harsh lights always reveal a harsher reality. Swan is not well. A new sore is beginning to appear on her lip, concealed with foundation and lipstick. Her nose is pinched, her hair brittle and not quite the right colour for her skin. Iglaf sees this and pities her, though in pitying her he pities himself. And seeing her straining for a sense of triumph against the weight of despair in her heart makes him love her again, or makes him think, at least, that they are alike, harbour the same paradoxes and aborted dreams.

He will hang about Swan, on these occasions, emitting guffaws of laughter, looking quite mad but full of a certain proprietary solicitude which does not escape her. Swan will feel Iglaf beside her in a way, she thinks, she has not felt him for years. He is overweight, too tanned, affects the same tweed jacket and the cap to hide his baldness. That smile is chiselled into his face, his manner is enthusiastic and unctuous. But she, too, all at once, feels a vast pity for his brave front. Swan suddenly remembers the boy Iglaf, how his naïveté, his abashed sweetness and embarrassed stoop once charmed her. And she thinks briefly that we fall in love with each other's failings, with our own vulnerabilities mirrored in the other.

She sees his sadness. Something too difficult to untangle comes into her heart. Everything is ruined, she thinks. The thought wars with her hardened facade, the contradictions rip through her. She too remembers the smell of burnt ticking, the feel of the bed sheet wrapped around her. Words like fate and history and love slip through her head but find no place to catch and hold. More and more, she has noticed, the words all seem spoken by someone else. Beyond the words, there exists only a mysterious emptiness. The feelings she recognizes as her own — shame, boredom, embarrassment, regret, resentment — remind her only that she once believed there was a message, but she has gotten it wrong. She suddenly feels panicky, lost in an endless regress of negation: she has gotten it wrong, but what if she is wrong about getting it wrong?

In her confusion, Swan reaches for Iglaf and touches his wrist protectively. Iglaf feels her touch and falls silent. The warmth of her hand seems a balm for all his wounds. The phrase "aborted dreams" sticks in his mind, and he remembers a dream from long ago, something about a book he had read or written. There is a thought, just on the tip of his tongue, he would like to tell Lily. But it is gone.

The Indonesian Client

THE INDONESIAN CLIENT was due at 2:15 p.m., in exactly ten minutes according to my watch. But Bove, the CEO, had taken suddenly and mysteriously ill over lunch and had failed to return to the office. This left myself and Janet Louth, my assistant, to handle the Indonesian client even though, till now, Bove had zealously and, as it seemed, short-sightedly arrogated all client relations to himself. Neither Janet nor I had ever seen a client, let alone conducted any of the intricate negotiations necessary for a sale. Nor were we at all experienced in the fine arts of wining and dining clients. Yes, of course, it was the wining and dining Bove loved. The wining and dining were no doubt responsible for his corpulence and for his sybaritic leer whenever I hinted at the advantages of my presence during a sale.

Bove was a man of the world and a philosopher; neither Janet nor I could make such a claim. Though Janet had long ago confided to me that she was the victim of a sexual addiction, neither of us counted this as worldliness so much as an aberration of her wounded innocence. And Janet was obese much the way Bove was, except that Bove carried himself with grace and delicacy while Janet kept a large plastic pig hanging from her key chain. "He's an animal," she once said, speaking of Bove, not the pig. "It's all a hunt for him." When she said things like this, she would blush and excuse herself to go to the ladies' room.

I myself was thin and hairless, the result of a childhood disease the nature of which my mother failed to explain before she died. I was, according to Bove, his idea man, a copywriter, a wordsmith (or, as I sometimes thought, simply a high-priced interlocutor with whom he could indulge his love of philosophical badinage). Our product did not speak for itself; on the other hand, I had never seen the product — I worked from technical specifications written by our engineers and looked to Bove for inspiration of a more practical and utilitarian nature. Bove, who was Dutch, had travelled briefly in the East and had a Zen approach to business which alternately fascinated and mystified me. He would wave his hand airily and say that any vagueness inherent in my copy could only help in selling the product to clients who, when they came to him, often did not know what they wanted, that the product, defined open-endedly, as it were, could mould itself to the desires of a client more absolutely than any single-use gadget of the more mundane variety.

Bove decried the sales philosophy of market niches; when he came to the plant after the takeover, he specifically charged our product development staff with the job of finding something we could build that would be niche-less and yet fill every niche. That this revolutionary concept was not easily embraced by, among others, the product development staff is attested to by the statistics: one suicide, one voluntary committal, four resignations, half a dozen forced retirements. Bove, in restructuring the department, committed funds for eighteen new hires of which only three — Montag, Straith and Naylor — survived their three-month probations.

The new product owed much to these three men, and yet I had never grown comfortable with them. They were evasive, edgy and paranoid. Montag, especially, had washed-out eyes of aquamarine which seemed to conceal some murderous intent. Janet, who blushingly confessed to having had sex with Naylor in a men's room toilet stall on two or three dozen occasions, said he was not even an engineer, that his previous experience consisted of selling ad slots for a CBS-TV affiliate in Norfolk, Virginia. According to Janet, Montag, Straith and Naylor reported independently to Bove, who encouraged them to compete with and even betray one another. She also said the engineering specifications I used to produce copy may have been falsified by one or all three in order to conceal from the others the true nature of their research. Add to this the fact that the product was built simultaneously in parts on eight production lines, each effectively sealed from the others by concrete walls, safety doors, air-locks and employee fraternization bans (there were separate dining and parking areas), and you can see that there was considerable backing for my theory that only Bove really knew what was going on in the plant.

But what did Bove know? I asked myself. And how was I to deal with Mr. Wahid, the Indonesian client soon to appear at the electronic surveillance gate which functioned as a reception area in front of the burnished steel doors of Bove's office? I switched on a bank of security video monitors which Bove had installed over Janet's desk and with some relief noted that the elevator remained empty and stationary at the bottom of its shaft. Above my head, an illuminated stock ticker flowed hypnotically like a ribbon of light around the walls of the room just beneath the ceiling. I noted with surprise a five-dollar uptick in our stock price and an equally sudden rise in volume over the morning lull.

Like myself, Janet is a Canadian. The plant, which housed our company headquarters, sprawled over fifty acres of a North Carolina industrial park just outside Winston-Salem. How we came here was nearly as much as mystery as the nature of our product itself — Janet Louth from North Battleford, Saskatchewan, I from Toronto, where I had edited trade magazines before a series of buyouts and job tenders sent me on an international tour: Brussels, Capetown, Vienna, San Remo, Kuala Lumpur and Winston-Salem. I had stock options in a company once called Trans-Ocean but since renamed eight times and now calling itself eTrans.com. When Bove arrived, he said I could stay, that he had had his eye on me since Vienna, that he preferred Canadians because, like the Dutch, they are culturally blank, an asset in modern business. Canadians are like suburban architecture, shopping malls and McDonald's franchises, he said. They are forerunners of the universal world culture.

Bove himself was large, bland and featureless. His white-blond hair and eyebrows, his Buddha-like corpulence, his strange, whispery voice (in which he affected an accurate but slight mid-western accent) seemed, all in all, to project what might be called a negative affect. That he preferred e-mail for in-plant communication went without saying. He liked to say that a document trail was worth a hundred decisions, and it was rumoured (Janet told me this) that he routinely had inter-office mail screened for key words or suspicious flow patterns he called vectors. What key words? I asked, trying to recall any incriminating diction I might have let slip in the past. Janet shrugged.

She was wearing a pair of silver earrings shaped like piglets which I had given her when we were still lovers, before Bove arrived. I do not say that we were in love then, only that some residual yearning for home drew us to one another. It is strange to think that being Canadian might influence what otherwise is a matter of hormones and genital reflex. But we were both a little lost in this weatherless new world of antiseptic pine barrens, featureless blue skies, gated communities for the new techno-elite (as we saw ourselves) and dust-free cutting edge industrial synergies. Janet had grown up on a hog farm on the bank of the North Saskatchewan River, highway of the ancient Indians, fur traders and imperial raiders; she remembered the harsh shrieks of dying pigs, her father's arms drenched in blood and the sight of a sow and her young frozen hard as rocks one cruel winter. Janet's sexual allure was all in the sudden, almost pathetic eagerness of her desire, while her desire itself was a combination of nostalgia for the glutinous blood-and-excrement-drenched mud of that distant river farm and her equally violent revulsion for a past she could not disown.

All sex, it seems to me, is the manipulation of guilt for pleasure. That Janet was aware of the compulsive sadness inherent in love goes without saying. She is an intelligent and perceptive young woman who yet could not help herself when the handsome and articulate foreigner, Bove, appeared so energetically upon the scene. (She claimed to have experienced a spontaneous orgasm as she watched him emerge from the gleaming, swept-back, erectile fuselage of the company Lear jet.) And it is a comment on Bove's insidious management practices that when he was finished with her, he reassigned Janet to me, so that all our relations would thenceforth be contaminated with triangularity, suspicion, jealousy and hatred. In a sense, this was simply an instance of the naked exercise of power symbolized by the exchange of women. But in my bitterness I perceived a subtle and perhaps more horrifying pattern. It was as if, as our product purified itself of mere functionality, we ourselves turned increasingly corrupt, petty and, yes, sinful, as though we were destined to sacrifice something of our humanity for the product to succeed.

Following another of Bove's injunctions, to hide nothing from me, Janet described sexual congress with our chief as "weird" and based on an anorgasmic latex fetish which involved Janet and Bove zipping themselves into identical rubber suits and breathing masks. Bove would then "doctor" Janet, that is, he would listen to her internal organs with a stethoscope until, encountering a heartbeat, he would throw off his mask and begin to weep. When she told me this, her cheeks blushed red with desire and humiliation, and she excused herself to go to the ladies' room. At that moment, I realized that she was lost to me, also that I was in love with her, and that the two propositions were identical.

. . .

Once I wanted to write the Great Canadian Novel. I had even composed the opening sentence: As they ate breakfast, it began to snow. Once I watched Saturday night hockey games on television with my father, dreamed of going to live on Baffin Island with the Eskimos and masturbated to fantasies of Jesuit martyrs writhing upon the stake. Once I slept with a sixteen-year-old figure skater named Paula Singleton, who simply and passionately opened her shirt for me one afternoon on her family room carpet. The world was a place of ambition, mystery and glory which somehow, in the years that followed, translated itself into senior editorships on *The Wool Newsletter*, *Canadian Sugar Beets Notes* and *The Northern Hog Growers Association Monthly*. (Admittedly, the latter did help me attract Janet's attention at the outset. Not everyone can casually interject: "Did you know that out of the 293 hog growers in Saskatchewan only 23% had the capitalization to introduce bulk feeding systems prior to 1995?")

At 2:15 precisely the elevator bell chimed and the UP light blinked on, though a glance at the video array showed me the elevator was still empty and stationary on the first floor. Janet noticed my furrow of concentration and sighed. Her chubby fingers swept over the keyboard and, abruptly, the video images shimmered and changed. Eight people boarded the elevator and began to ascend, even as the elevator doors slid open and a solitary black man in an orange eTrans.com maintenance uniform emerged into the arbour of security sensors. I recognized him immediately as one of a crew of state-sponsored employees hired from a local home to enhance the company's image of social responsibility. Another screen showed Bove seated at his monolithic desk speaking into a wireless phone; another showed Janet working industriously at her computer; another showed me urinating in the men's room; and yet another showed Bove inspecting the shop floor in the company of Montag, Straith and Naylor, all clad, somewhat comically given their self-important attitudes, in anti-dust, anti-static suits.

Evidently, and no doubt at Bove's insistence, even our security apparatus had been turned into a beacon of internal disinformation. Again, as had happened increasingly in the past months, I asked myself, What is real? Why am I here? What is the purpose of all my work? Was Bove really ill? How much did Janet know? What is love? Perhaps nothing, aside from the image of Janet pursued by Bove in a rubber outfit and stethoscope, had shaken my faith in the routine trustworthiness of things more than this display of out-and-out fabrication. Although my faith in Bove as a brilliant, if eccentric, business manager remained unshaken, I now realized I would never be privy to his system, that I would always be manipulated and never manipulate, that my sense of self would always be secondary to someone else's sense of me, that reality was someone else's perspective. The screens shimmered once more on Janet's signal, and a new set of equally false images appeared. I looked at her aghast, and she shrugged, causing the little piglets dangling from her ears to bobble seductively.

But I had no time to consider this development because the maintenance man, trapped in a web of automatic safety gates, was waving energetically in our direction. When Bove was on watch, the office systems worked perfectly — yes, it occurred to me now that possibly, in his Zen-like detachment, he simply turned everything off. It took a few minutes, but we finally extricated the maintenance man with no more damage than a superficial radiation burn on his left hand because he would, against all advice, attempt to view parts of himself in the bomb detection unit. His name was Harley, I remembered now. I had seen him in several of our commercials, posing as a typical eTrans.com employee and spokesperson, symbol of the democratic benevolence emanating from the new product.

We sat him at Janet's desk before the video array, which captured his attention immediately. It was now 2:30 and evident that Mr. Wahid was either delayed or had skipped his appointment or did not exist. Both Janet Louth and I began to experience an existential vertigo, the effect of trying to divine Bove's intentions when his prime intention was always to conceal his intentions. His absence, coupled with Mr. Wahid's failure to appear on schedule, now seemed dense with implication. With Harley, we remained glued to the video array, watching events we knew were not taking place, even catching ourselves from time to time performing actions we could not remember having performed. Harley, who had clearly achieved some Zen state himself, was not bothered by this at all; somehow he had already accepted the completely fictional nature of reality.

I considered whiling away the time with my usual work, though the thought of translating falsified technical summaries into fact sheets, instruction manuals and promotional brochures now seemed, frankly, a waste of time. On the ticker, eTrans.com was up eight points, volume was surging. Suddenly, it occurred to me that Indonesia had once been a Dutch colony, that there was at least an associative as well as a historical link between Bove and Mr. Wahid. What this meant, I did not know.

In Canada, snow was falling. Snow was falling generally on the great northern lakes, on the western mountains, on the glaciers crouched over Baffin Island, on the cedars bordering the slough where Janet lost her virginity to a boy named Michael F. who sang in the church choir and caught the flu from her, on the empty streets of Toronto, on the statues of Victoria and Sir John A. Macdonald in Queen's Park. I had once had a bitter fantasy that one day snow would begin to fall and never stop and that the whole continent, down to about Cincinnati, would disappear under the awful weight of a new Ice Age.

Yes, I will not gainsay the fact that Canada had become a symbol of everything about myself I wished to leave behind, that my constant dream of snow, glaciers and, occasionally, amnesia was a childish dream of grace and redemption, that all Canadians know the true meaning of Original Sin, of not being among the Elect.

(My parents were Presbyterians, my degree was in English and Theology — I was bound to speak this way on occasion.)

An hour passed at eTrans.com (now eighteen dollars above its record high). Janet passed much of this time nervously rushing to the bathroom, a sign that she was succumbing to her addiction. In her eyes, her rubicund cheeks, her shaking hands, one could see the humiliation, the almost voluptuous submission to her weakness. Harley and I played two-handed bridge for stock options while watching the video array, which, when you watched it carefully, presented nothing more than a randomly repetitive sequence of ten-minute video loops.

There was something disturbingly inept and shoddy about the thinness of the illusion. Bove had counted on carelessness, boredom and inattention to collaborate with him in fostering this fake reality. And, of course, he had succeeded. The fact of my own unwitting collusion struck me with the force of a religious revelation just as Harley (who had turned out to be something of an idiot savant at cards) took the last trick and relieved me of $500,000 from my retirement fund. He kept chortling to himself, saying over and over, "Who's the dummy now?" Though it was all in good humour, and I had grown to like and admire him as a sort of natural man whose impulses, judgements and perceptions were all unmediated by ulterior motive or outside influence.

I still believed in the product, mind you. And Bove. But nothing else was what it seemed. And possibly it was only belief I believed in. In other words, I still believed things must make sense, and the only way anything made sense was if I believed Bove had some reason for all the manipulation and fakery at eTrans.com. There was a product, we sold untold millions of units, capital expansion continued at an incredible rate, shareholder value increased as the stock went up, split and rose again.

Admittedly, the company was still unprofitable. In fact, the steady seepage at the bottom line had lately become a hemorrhage of red ink. But this did not discourage investors, who flocked in ever-growing numbers to buy our stock. I myself had played some small part in this — following Bove's suggestion, I had written a series of press releases outlining a company policy that put expansion before profit, implying that it was Bove's sagacious plan to lose massive amounts of money now to ensure future profits that would be proportionally greater, that the huge losses at eTrans.com somehow actually guaranteed future profitability. At the time, I believed this. After all, we had created a product that everyone wanted. But what was the product?

At that moment, as if in answer to my unspoken question, Janet Louth re-emerged from the ladies' room, this time completely naked. She was huge, a Canadian Venus of Willendorf. In the crook of one arm, she carried a fuzzy stuffed pig; from the other hand, she dragged a dolphin-blue rubber suit made of latex as thin as those ultra-thin condoms. She was weeping, her great breasts heaved like tectonic plates. She was clearly in a paroxysm of desire or a crisis of faith or the afterglow of some primal orgasm or all three. Her eyes were glassy, she seemed unaware of our presence.

Harley muttered, "Wow." Then, "Fuck me, Mama." Which I took to be his ur-reading of the situation. I myself, naturally, wanted to go deeper. Janet and I had been lovers once. I had seen her naked before, but never so naked as now, if you see what I mean. Her nakedness now — under the full-spectrum gas tubes Bove insisted upon — seemed shocking, ancient, unutterably painful and yet achingly innocent. Women, as was ever evident in Janet's case, are pure signs, objects of desire whose desire is all that is desired of them. It has always been difficult in our culture to see women as anything but two-dimensional, as having souls or even brains. Even now, when women have been accorded a certain grudging place in society, evidence of female thinking is often greeted with nothing more than irritable forbearance. "Yes, yes, my dear, always interesting to hear from the women in the audience, but as I was saying..."

All at once, I began to wonder what Janet actually thought,

trailing that disgraceful carapace of passion. What secret knowledge had been vouchsafed her in the sanctum of the eTrans.com executive ladies' room? What did she think of me? Of my hairlessness? Of love? How had she been convinced to conspire with Bove to doctor the security video array? Like Bove, she seemed to be hiding something; in her nakedness, more now than ever.

It occurred to me suddenly that some of my earlier inferences might be faulty. With a sickening sense of déjà vu, I realized that I had believed in what was hidden simply because it was hidden, and, hence, that I had all along somehow put more faith in the thing that I did not know (because it was hidden) than in the thing that was right before my eyes. Hell, I simply discounted what was before my eyes. I had fallen for the fallacy of interpretation; I had been living inside a poem. (Hence Plato's famous distrust of poets — Bove was fond of quoting Plato, whom he considered a superior sort of public relations flack for what was then the new technology of writing.)

It was 3 p.m. The markets would be open another hour; eTrans.com had gone through the roof, as they say. I had been watching CNN the last fifteen minutes, giggling softly to myself. A voluptuous young woman with a sensual overbite and eyes darting behind too much mascara spoke from the floor of the New York Stock Exchange. Rumour of Asian takeover interest in eTrans.com ("Meetings are being held as I speak," she said) had sparked a feverish rally during an otherwise sleepy trading day. Surging volume had twice tripped the New York Stock Exchange circuit breakers, creating artificial stoppages which only seemed to increase demand. Institutional buying was strong; fund managers, usually imperturbable in a crisis, were frantically scrambling to turn cash reserves into equity; the eTrans.com rocket was dragging the whole market upwards. Three times the announcer mentioned that

Indonesia was a vast country made up of many islands, the third most populous nation in the world. Once or twice, I thought the phrase "shadow puppets" was on the tip of her tongue.

Harley was watching *Nickelodeon* on another screen. Elsewhere eight people boarded the elevator on the first floor, Bove spoke into his wireless phone. Phones rang in every corner of the office, message lights blinked. At my own network terminal, the little arm on the mailbox was up. Was Bove trying to reach us? The stock ticker whirled about our heads like a giant halo, now largely ignored because CNN was transmitting real-time eTrans.com quotes in an on-screen box.

Janet worried me. She seemed somehow vacant, if not quite mad. I had wrapped her in a bath towel retrieved from the executive spa and sauna off Bove's office. The towel was imperial purple with the eTrans.com logo in gold thread. Janet knelt at my feet, shivering or shuddering, her body wracked by desire or unspoken terrors, cuddling her pig, talking to herself. From time to time, I caught the words, "Piggy needs to get out of here. It's not safe. Something terrible is going to happen. Piggy needs to get out." The sound of her voice, the nagging little you-have-mail icon, the ringing phones, the thought of the missing Indonesian client and the equally absent Bove triggered a wave of paranoia in me that warred against the redemptive digital read-out in the CNN box. "We're rich," I kept repeating, the words consoling me like a mantra.

A sober-minded commentator came on in a network cutaway to remind us of eTrans.com's record losses in the last quarter and read a company warning (which I did not recall writing) of increased losses in the current quarter. But then he went on to say (yes, with a messianic gleam in his insane eyes) that there was no arguing with the market, which had clearly shaken off conventional worries about eTrans.com's balance sheet. "The market is never wrong," he said. "What we are witnessing is history in the making, nothing short of the birth of a new economy, a mechanism we will only come to understand in retrospect. Money is being sucked into the market like air into a tornado. Any man, woman or child who can beg, borrow or steal a buck is putting it into eTrans.com this afternoon."

I could almost hear the pneumatic sound of money, money everywhere being sucked into the vacuum of desire. I felt a chill. The hair on my neck would have stood if I'd had any. And I realized the eerie unreality of it all, the suck and whoosh of money being hoovered out of pension funds, retirement plans, endowments, charity trusts, college funds, rainy day accounts, nest eggs, mattresses, cookie jars, piggy banks, all of that cold, hard cash transforming into electrons and digital readouts.

Suddenly I wanted to get out, too. Janet's words had somehow seeped beneath my conscious thoughts and re-emerged as my own. I needed to get out. Of what? I asked myself. The market? Surely I could sell my stock in an instant and retire fabulously wealthy, even with the losses I had sustained to Harley during our bridge game earlier in the afternoon. But the thought sickened me. Somewhere inside I could sense an electronic buzz of desire searing my brain. I wanted to turn it off completely. Merely succeeding, merely being wealthy, I realized, would never quiet the buzz. I had ceased, you realize, to think; my mind was a clutter of strobe-like images: the digital spiral of eTrans.com's stock price, Janet's naked, shuddering flesh, Dad's face in the moon-glow of the television so long ago. I realized it was the stock quote box, steadily clicking upward like an odometer, that was driving out thought. Replacing thought, I felt a painful, balloon-like burgeoning of what at first I took to be hope but which I suddenly realized was desire itself, an open-ended, ever more voracious need dragging me into the future. That little box on the screen looked like nothing less than the grave itself.

At 3:18 p.m., again suddenly (everything was moving forward with a jerky immediacy, as if time itself had been digitized), the CNN picture changed, and there was Bove himself, not ill at all, but looking relaxed, fat and avuncular in an open-necked shirt and suit jacket. Wind blew through his wispy white-blond hair. Behind him, the sea stretched into a sunlit distance. His face wore an attentive, amused expression as he listened to the commentator's gushing introduction: how in a single hour Bove's personal wealth had exceeded that of all the great computer entrepreneurs of the eighties and nineties, how the Gateses and the Allens and the Cases were nothing but forerunners and footnotes, how it had been his gift to see the next great technological wave and catch its crest.

Then Bove began to speak. "I cannot comment at this time on the rumours involving our Indonesian client, but I can say that Indonesia, the third largest nation in the world in terms of population, is extremely important to our growth strategy. We are a small company, just coming back after the recent takeover and restructuring. But we have been blessed with an impressive product development team and a future-oriented marketing philosophy. We are entering the post-technology, post-Internet era, when all the rules that were broken in the past five years will simply be broken again, only more quickly. Since the invention of the personal computer, there has been a geometric trend: products have become better and cheaper at an ever-increasing rate. The time lag between one revolutionary change and the next has decreased with a regularity that has stunned many of the pundits. But one only need accept these new assumptions, say, as a new kind of natural law, and the future becomes radiantly clear."

As Bove spoke, the eTrans.com stock price clicked relentlessly higher. The Dow and the S&P 500 were nosing down, first tentatively, then more steeply.

"My God," said Janet, shivering in her eTrans.com bath towel, "they're dumping blue chips to buy eTrans."

"Are you all right?" I asked, relieved and actually surprised to hear something like a normal voice coming from Janet's lips.

This calm new voice had a comforting, down-to-earth timbre. You could hear the quiet, muddy waters of the North Saskatchewan

River in that voice. She reached and took my hand in hers, a gesture which brought tears to my eyes.

I squeezed her cold fingers almost violently in a reciprocal gesture of affection. And it suddenly occurred to me that love is an impure emotion, that it somehow takes into account all the failures, betrayals and inconsistencies in the lover, that it is not love if it does not accept and forgive the humanity of the other. Precisely what this meant I was not sure, but it produced in me a mixed feeling of sadness, generosity and warmth. I knew that something flowed between Janet and me at that moment that cancelled the images of latex sex with Bove and bathroom sex with Naylor and countless other flagrant spasms of delight with nameless partners, not to mention my own cool detachment and fastidiousness, which I saw now as an attitude of superiority born of fear and vengefulness.

On the screen, Bove had stopped talking while the interviewer posed another question. But the network had lost the interviewer's sound feed, and Bove seemed to be listening to something else altogether, the sound of light moving, or that mystical wind stirred up by the billions of electronic dollars swirling around the Earth toward the New York Stock Exchange, or the rustling background noise of the universe, the great Om of God talking.

Abruptly, the network cut away and the CNN stock floor bimbo came on the screen, weeping like a child, mascara streaming down her cheeks. "Something's wrong," she moaned. "I'm scared. I'm so scared. It's not supposed to be like this." Then she grasped her microphone in both hands, shut her eyes and began to recite in the squeaky voice of a terrified eight-year-old, "Now I lay me down to sleep. I pray the Lord my soul to keep."

Behind her the stock exchange floor turned strangely quiet; traders, superseded by electronic trading programs, stood in awe, watching the numbers swirl around them like flames, watching their doom. And I recalled Bove waxing philosophical about the great bull market of the 1990s, how, he said, the stock boom was a direct result of Nietzsche's dictum "God is dead," which had also led to surrealism, postmodernism, MTV and the abandonment of the gold standard. "When Nietzsche unlinked God from the Word, he began a process of divergence: ideas which had once seemed connected began to drift apart. Signs separated from meaning, and money, which always had a syntax of its own, separated from value. And it became easier and easier to sense the inscrutable forces which drive existence, the backdrop of our illusions."

I shuddered now to think what he meant: the infinite, endless, oceanic desire of which each of us was but an expression, a minute incarnation — yes, the self as an ephemeral concretization of the World Greed, which Bove had understood so well. It was 3:33 p.m., and the New York Stock Exchange circuit breakers had tripped a third time. The numbers in the little eTrans.com box stopped rising. A well-known CNN anchorwoman came on with a series of news briefs: rioting had broken out in a number of American cities, a dozen states had mobilized National Guard units, right-wing militia groups across the country had notified members to arm themselves and proceed to collection points, politicians everywhere were telling people to calm themselves, which naturally had the effect of increasing hysteria. Yet the anchorwoman's words momentarily lulled me. Yes, I thought, words still did work, still described reality, still knit up the dangling threads of cosmic despair.

And then, inexorably, the numbers began to rise again. Fifteen minutes remained in the trading day, but one had the distinct impression that, on this day like no other, trading would not stop. Mechanisms put in place to ensure the easy flow of capital around the world would somehow keep the stock in play. As the New York Stock Exchange closed, another market somewhere else would open, and another, and another, following the movement of the sun, the flow of time itself.

What was the product? I asked myself. What was it Montag, Naylor and Straith had slaved so secretly to invent? What was it the eight production lines ran night and day with invariant efficiency to build? What mystery did the falsified engineering specs, those runic glyphs, conceal?

"We should leave," I said. The office, the whirling stock ticker, the flickering screens signalled a reality that suddenly seemed toxic.

"Where are we going, boss?" asked Harley, the perfect image of my black other, dusky, obedient and trusting. I had not even meant to include him, but now I knew I must — the world was teaching me.

"Yes, where?" asked Janet, whose desire I had desired as crudely and insanely as any Bove or Naylor. When would I see my friends as anything but a projection of my own dysfunctional dreams? When would my stories bloom with real people? And was there a reality beyond the digitized images of my fantasies?

"Baffin Island," I said, "as far north as we can get, way up in Canada."

I knew it was essential to remain focused and decisive. Even as I said the words, my eyes caught the upward-clicking numbers on the eTrans.com box, and, briefly, I wondered if I was doing the right thing, or if the market would redeem me. My God, the riches we were leaving behind. And yet they seemed inconsequential as dust. The Earth turned, the continents shifted, the vast currents of ocean and air churned as endlessly and meaninglessly as desire itself. I no longer wished to be redeemed into that nothingness of pure motion and greed. I wanted love and work and friendship — old things. I didn't even know if they existed.

Would we survive? I didn't care. I claimed that necessity for my own. Janet tottered back to the ladies' room to retrieve her clothes. She left the latex suit in the trash like an old self. Harley went to telephone his mother and find his tool belt, which he thought might come in handy on Baffing Island, as he called it. I reached to turn off the security array before the market close. Just as I did so, a strange little man with dark skin, large glasses and a round brimless hat something like a Turkish fez appeared to enter the elevator on the ground floor. He nervously checked his watch as the screen went dead.

The stock ticker still swirled about my head, but I ignored it, putting my desk in order one last time (old habits die hard). I thought of leaving a message for Bove, something like "Pull the plug — save yourself!" but decided not to. He would understand, he was the master of absences and knew their manifold meanings. Perhaps, I thought, he never intended to return anyway.

Janet came back from the ladies' room, looking girlish and fresh, which I didn't understand until I realized she had taken off her makeup as well. She looked cured of her addiction, though I knew human nature well enough not to trust this perception and forgave her just the same.

Harley had abandoned his orange maintenance uniform and was wearing neat khaki cargo pants, a polo shirt, a golf jacket and a look of ironic amusement which made him seem, suddenly, intelligent.

What was I going to leave behind? I wondered. I took out my wallet, bulging with IDs, licences, credit cards, debit cards, ATM cards, even cash, and set it atop my computer monitor. I placed my Rolex next to it in an afflatus of television-style romanticism.

We passed Mr. Wahid on the way to the elevator. He was struggling within the arbour of security sensors, answering computer-generated questions designed to establish identity and purpose of visit. When we cracked the weather doors to the outside, the air felt suddenly like air. Janet, looking buxom and good-hearted — that is to say, beautiful — linked her arm in mine and took Harley by the hand. Vast distances beckoned us. Harley thought the walk would do us good. At our backs, I still heard the ghostly hiss of money like the beating of a billion unseen wings, but Harley insisted it was just the wind in the pines. Maybe it was.

The Left Ladies Club

I

THREE YEARS AGO, when I was already pregnant with the twins, my husband Duffy quit his job as an English teacher at the Ragged Point high school to become a novelist. At first, nothing much changed. It was summer vacation so Duffy was supposed to be home anyway. He moved the bed and chifforobe out of the guest bedroom and moved in a desk and a new colour TV.

After the first week or so, the novel began to go badly. Duffy started to drink for inspiration, taking a cooler of Mexican beer up to the guest bedroom each morning. But the novel only got worse.

Duffy started going to the local bars at night so he could meet real people he could put in his novel. Every two weeks on Tuesday nights, he went to a writers' group because he needed to be with other artists, people who thought and talked the way he did. He met another novelist there named Tammy Cudrup.

Tammy Cudrup had had quite a life. She had been in the poetry business before turning to novels. The poetry had made her husband envious and turned him into nothing but a vindictive vessel of violence, or so she put it. She went to a priest for counselling, but evidently the priest had misunderstood the vow of chastity because he took advantage of her in a moment of weakness. He also said it would be less of a sin if they just didn't do it the normal way.

She then lived in Biloxi with a drug-addicted person who claimed to be a sculptor. Their house was furnished with rocks and stolen home electronics equipment. Tammy herself had a little go-around with drugs during this period, but she told Duffy she had licked the problem.

After the sculptor, she spent some time in an institution over at Baton Rouge, though she was never specific about what kind of institution it was. A young black attendant there would come around at night and strap her to her bed and use her body. Tammy said there was nothing she could do about it. The doctors refused to believe anything like this could happen.

Her novel was about how her father molested her when she was a child, how he threatened to kill her pet puppy if she told. The climax of the novel was a scene involving the heroine and a junior high school basketball team in which she had what Duffy called an epiphany.

Tammy had Clorox-blond hair and a beauty mark on her left cheek. Evidently, by the time Duffy told me all the above, Tammy had already given him several epiphanies of his own.

I misinterpreted Duffy's good mood in those days as a sign of an unexpected upturn in the novel-writing business. At the dinner table, I would pass cheerful little remarks about how nice it would be to meet Burt Reynolds when they made the movie. The twins were kicking and we were behind in the mortgage payments, but Duffy's spirits had never been higher. He was growing one of those little goatee beards.

He decided to rent the vacant floor above Rance's Menswear on Water Street so he could have what he called a real studio loft. He needed space, he said, gesturing with his arms. He needed an artistic atmosphere to nurture his creative ideas.

Duffy's new novel — in those days, he still read me the pages he was satisfied with — was about a boy named Scuffy whose father molests him on a manure pile behind the barn. Stricken by guilt, the father beats his young, pregnant wife to death, only to die himself moments later beneath the hooves of a stampeding herd of Jersey cows.

I made Duffy mad by telling him I thought he ought to research the cow thing.

Duffy's real father is a kindly, golf-playing druggist in Vancleave, the next town upstate from Ragged Point. He's been married to Duffy's mother for twenty-nine years. They square dance and cook Cajun for hobbies, and every summer they drive west in their Wanderhome to take courses at Oral Roberts University in Tulsa.

On the back of the Wanderhome there is a red, white and blue bumper sticker which reads HAPPY TOGETHER, HAPPY FOREVER, AT PEACE IN THE HANDS OF THE LORD. Duffy's father made that up himself and had thousands of the bumper stickers printed so he could hand them out free in the drugstore or to people they met on their summer trips.

I told Duffy I thought it might hurt his parents' feelings to see themselves written up as homicidal, incest-practising pedophiles.

Duffy got writer's block bad after that. He bought a hunting rifle over at Brent Wardlow's hardware store and took to sitting for hours on end in front of the TV in the middle of that empty studio loft, clicking the safety on and off, just staring and clicking and sipping Corona from the cooler by his chair.

I know this because I went up there one day to check after Duffy's sister Wenda dropped by to say her husband Will had seen Duffy and Tammy Cudrup drinking coffee together at the Dunkin' Donut three afternoons in the last week.

When Duffy saw me coming up the stairs, he just glared. He said he didn't want me bothering him when he was writing.

I could see well enough he was watching women's beach volleyball from Venice, California, on the Sports Network.

He said writers often got their best ideas when they seemed to be doing nothing, and their spouses and loved ones ought to learn to understand that.

Click, click went that safety.

I said maybe Tammy Cudrup was better at understanding the connection between literary genius and beach volleyball than a person's own wife.

Duffy said maybe it was time to realize that we'd grown apart, that while he had been expanding his intellectual horizons, I had remained a simple Ragged Point girl with nothing but babies, living room sets and singing in the Bethel Baptist Church choir on my mind.

I said what do you mean? Do you mean I got pregnant with twins all by myself? Or maybe that I'm carrying Jesus H. Christ and his brother inside my stomach?

Duffy said I was getting excited.

I said excited? Why should I be excited? I am speaking with a man who drinks coffee at the Dunkin' Donut for a living and thinks that pregnancy causes brain death.

That night Duffy moved into the studio loft for good.

A week later, Levon Rance evicted him because in Ragged Point the upstairs storage area above a menswear store is not zoned for residential use.

Duffy moved into a trailer on the west side of town by the sewage lagoon with another novelist named Edgar Demming.

2

ON THE WHOLE, going into labour, driving myself to the Ragged Point Hospital in a car with a nervous carburetor and delivering two five-and-a-half-pound babies was no more intolerable than having red-hot spikes driven through my eyeballs.

This was a month after Duffy left.

I called them Rachel and Raghib — Rachel for my Ma who died in a freak auto accident involving a Palmetto Fruit Company delivery van on the I-10 interchange when I was thirteen, and Raghib for my doctor, Dr. Raghib Natwal, a recent immigrant to the United States.

Duffy's parents, his sister Wenda, my Pa and my brother Garnet were all in the waiting room for the blessed event, but evidently Duffy was unable to break away from the rigors of novel-writing to check in on his family.

Duffy's father was so disappointed that he threw the two dozen HAPPY TOGETHER bumper stickers he'd brought to hand around at the hospital into the trash. He said the words somehow just didn't seem to ring true anymore.

Wenda said Duffy had started a new book. The hero was a man named Cuffy who wants to be a painter but lives in a part of the country where art is not appreciated. Fired from his job, reviled by his family and hounded by former friends and newspaper critics, he perseveres with his craft and eventually becomes rich and famous in New York.

His wife begs him to take her back, but he has formed an eternal bond with a drug-addicted model who inspires his best work but dies of an overdose of methadone while trying to kick her heroin habit.

Wenda said her husband Will had seen Tammy Cudrup in the company of Edgar Demming several afternoons at the Dunkin' Donut, crying and carrying on.

If you asked her, she said, the whole novel-writing crowd was a little spooky.

When I got home from the hospital, there were two dozen sweetheart roses from Dr. Natwal waiting in the nursery (formerly Duffy's study).

Rachel had the croup. Raghib had what I was certain would prove to be amoebic dysentery but which Dr. Natwal called loose stool. For the first few weeks, I tended just to sit in tears in the Naugahyde recliner staring out the picture window with the babies tugging at my breasts.

I don't believe I got to keep my shirt on more than fifteen minutes at a time in those days.

Dr. Natwal came by three times a day and generally stayed through the evening, playing Bach and some weird Indian sitar music on CDs to the kids and entertaining them by making animals out of pieces of string.

He was plainly in love with me, though I could not understand why anyone could be anything but repelled by a hysterical woman with leaking milk jugs dangling from her chest and baby poop in her hair.

Anyway I was too distracted to give any but the most passing attention to this development.

Duffy's parents did their best to help out. His mother would change Little Raghib (I had started calling them Big Raghib and Little Raghib) and do the wash.

Duffy's father sat in the living room, snapping rubber bands and running his fingers through his thinning crewcut. Religion and family values had taken a terrible beating, as far as he was concerned, at the hands of his own son. And, though he was invariably courteous to Dr. Natwal, the presence of a coloured man in my house caused him no end of consternation.

When his children were well into their third month, Duffy was jailed in Biloxi on a charge of vagrancy.

The story I got from Wenda (Duffy was coming around to their house for the occasional home-cooked meal now, which Wenda gave him out of pity) was that Duffy, Edgar, Tammy and a black man named Earl Shootis had driven to Biloxi for a poetry reading at the public library in a car Earl had borrowed from a man known only as Woodrow.

Tammy Cudrup said she had never heard anything so beautiful and wept noisily throughout the presentation, including the library announcements.

When it was over, she spilled coffee on the poet and set a small fire in the waste basket with a lit cigarette butt. Then she and the poet disappeared in Woodrow's car, leaving Duffy, Edgar and Earl Shootis to fend for themselves.

Duffy, Edgar and Earl drank a dozen Coronas at a Negro bar called Bennie's Black Heaven waiting for Tammy, and then fell asleep behind a palmetto next to the Confederate War Memorial, where the Biloxi deputy found them at ten o'clock the next morning.

Apparently, an alert public defender plea-bargained the original charges down to vagrancy, and the Ragged Point literary crowd got off with fines and weekend sentences.

Tammy showed up three days later minus Woodrow's car, still dressed in her poetry reading clothes, with her wrist in a cast and a black eye.

Wenda said Duffy looked like death warmed over, and she suspected drugs were involved.

He had started on a prison novel called *Hard Time* in which an innocent young New York art photographer named Ruffy, hitch-hiking through the South, finds himself railroaded into a brutal prison farm by the sadistic town sheriff after the sheriff's flirtatious daughter makes a pass at him.

Fellow inmates gang-rape Ruffy, then beat him nearly to death for sharing his food with an elderly, blind black man. When prison snitches finger him for the murder of a hated guard named Killer Muldoon, Ruffy's sentence is increased to life without parole.

Over the years, working in the prison shop, Ruffy invents and builds a filmless camera that allows him to record conditions behind the walls. This leads to liberal government reforms of prison life, which come too late for the young photographer, who dies at the hands of yet another would-be rapist.

I tried to call Duffy when I heard about his law trouble, but Southern Bell had disconnected Edgar Demming's phone for non-payment.

I took Big Raghib's car and left him with the kids and drove out of town on Water Street to the sewage lagoon to see for myself.

Duffy was sitting in front of the trailer in a lawn chair with a burst seat, staring at the weeds along the sewage lagoon fence through a pair of cheap sunglasses with the ear pieces taped on.

He looked thinner than when he had left. Somebody had shot holes through the wall and roof of the trailer, and one window had a month-old *Times-Picayune* taped over a broken spot.

Two mongrel dogs, looking more dead than alive, stretched in the dry dirt at Duffy's feet.

When I got out of the car, I could hear someone typing furiously inside the trailer.

I said I was glad to catch him on a break.

Duffy stared at me through his glasses and took a drag on a homemade cigarette, which he held between nicotine-stained fingers that shook so hard he knocked ashes down the front of his shirt without noticing.

I said it must be tough to find time for himself, what with all the editors and agents calling him, not to mention movie producers, Hollywood stars and the entertainment media, and what about that segment on *Lifestyles of the Rich and Famous*, anyway?

I was also real sorry he'd missed the Pulitzer Prize again this year, but what did silly old judges know anyhow?

Duffy said nothing.

The typing stopped, and presently muffled rifle shots could be heard coming from inside the trailer. A couple of new holes suddenly appeared in the aluminum roof near the ventilator shaft over the kitchenette.

Duffy barely moved, but his face took on a wary, hunted expression. I was suddenly so confused by the coincidence of sadness, remembered love, sewage lagoons and broken down trailer homes that I lost my head. I bent down abruptly, kissed his cheek, then ran to the car, didn't look back.

Six months later I had an ill-advised yet breathtaking romance with a man named Jethron Ord who had a swashbuckling air and a mean eye and travelled in farm equipment and underwater weed harvesters. For a little over three weeks, I neglected my babies, failed to return my in-laws' phone calls, skipped choir practice and spent several afternoons a week in badly air-conditioned motel rooms down the coast, swashbuckling around in my underwear and drinking large amounts of Rebel Yell in Dixie cups.

I do not believe I ever felt so wicked or so good. I loved the way I looked in the bathroom mirrors in the dim green glow of the strip lights, with my lipstick smudged like a bruise, my hair mussed and my bra straps falling off my shoulders. Words like "torpid," "bestial," "damp" and "licentious" seemed suddenly to belong to me in a peculiar and sensual way. And when it was over, when Jethron left town to return to Nashville and his lips-like-whips lawyer wife and their three near-sighted daughters under the age of five, he seemed wrung-out, dazed and regretful, which I took as a compliment.

3

ONE DAY THERE WAS a knock at the door, and when I opened it, I found Tammy Cudrup weeping on the concrete porch. She was wearing a black teddy under a denim shirt open to her waist and carried a dirty white canvas bag with the words WRITE A BOOK FOR JESUS in black letters.

She asked could she come in, and I said why the Hell not you took my husband and would you like the keys to the car too?

She said she wouldn't come in if I was going to be hostile.

The word hostile and the way she drew herself up when she said it gave me the giggles. I said why surely, Tammy, I would love for you to come in. Which she did.

Rachel and Little Raghib were three. I worked the reception desk for Dr. Natwal's practice. We had an old-fashioned dinner-and-dancing friendship that periodically threatened to slide into something more serious but always managed not to. Duffy had found work part-time as a groundskeeper for the school board. Mornings, driving the kids to the babysitter, I would see him patrolling the concrete paths with his edger and a tank of Roundup in a backpack, looking like a scuba diver with a harpoon gun. He was tan and lean and didn't shave but once every three or four days, which gave him one of those attractive I-don't-give-a-damn looks.

Even Wenda said she'd never seen a man wear failure so well. But then, she added, he doesn't have anything else to do all day but walk around in the sun and look after himself. Wenda had grown bitter due to the fact that her husband Will, once a shooting star in the field of claims adjustment, was plateauing out in lower middle management.

Edgar Demming had sold a screenplay to the movies and checked himself into a rehab clinic in Baton Rouge. Earl Shootis had published a book of poems and found a job teaching writing at a small liberal arts college in the northeast where they needed a black poet on account of their institutional commitment to hiring minorities, cripples, immigrants and women (I was glad to see we had not lost our traditional position down there among the dregs of society). Tammy Cudrup had written three Christian romance novels under the pen name Wallis de Vere and appeared twice on the Christian Network to tell how God inspired her to write. It's like having a spiritual orgasm, she said. And the *Times-Picayune* had run a feature on the Ragged Point literary scene complete with photographs of the trailer by the sewage lagoon, the Dunkin' Donut and Tammy in a tasteful dress that showed her cleavage and belly-button ring.

According to Wenda, Duffy was working on a new novel about an elderly pensioner named Muffy Doyle who lives in a cabin at the edge of town and does nothing, except people notice that good things seem to happen when he's around. Muffy never says a word, but the neighbours just know he's amazingly wise. By the time he dies — sitting in his rocking chair, looking out at the Gulf — they have come to realize he is a saint amongst them, an angel sent to make the world a better place.

That's not the way it really ends, said Tammy, sitting on my chaise, balancing a cup of coffee and a Dunkin' Donut on her lap. He wrote a last chapter where the townspeople discover body parts buried all over the property. Muffy Doyle turns out to have been a psycho killer the whole time, and now everyone knows where all those pet dogs and black children were disappearing to.

She couldn't understand why I found this so funny. It's real sad, she said.

She looked sweet and eager to please but with a fragile dignity — men see this in a woman and translate it as: good-hearted, filthy in bed.

She said she and Duffy were just friends now, that all he talked about was broad-leaf herbicides, watering cycles and the difficulties of aging underground sprinkler systems.

She said she had come to me because she thought I might be the only person who could understand her. I took this to mean I was the only person left in Ragged Point she hadn't tried at one time or another, or that somehow sleeping with the same novelist made us almost like kin. Also something regrettable had occurred at Reverend Jakin's house the night before after the weekly pancake and prayer supper when Reverend Jakin's wife and the kids were in St. Louis visiting his in-laws. It was bound to come out.

She began to weep again with gusto, as if her whole world had just caved in, like my Rachel when life has disappointed her in some particular way. I showed Tammy the bathroom, then made up the daybed in the Florida room and dropped the blinds. She fell asleep with her thumb in her mouth as soon as she put her head on the pillow, though it was only eleven a.m.

I telephoned Duffy, and then reporters started to call, reporters who mistook me for Tammy because she had left my number with the desk sergeant after they booked Reverend Jakin. After the third call, I started pretending to be Tammy Cudrup: No, sir, it was a complete surprise to me. He was my minister and spiritual advisor. He forced me to do everything and shout bad words against the Lord. Yes, it's true, I was wearing nothing to speak of when I escaped and flagged down Cissy Delman's husband Bubba, who gave me his shirt and kept his eyes averted, praise the Lord. Beyond that I have no comment. I will not tell you what I am wearing now.

I feel like I am in a story, I said when Duffy came over. Is she always like this?

He didn't say anything, just blinked and stared at the kitchen walls as if walls were some new thing. He smelled of fresh sweat and grass clippings, and his cheeks were red from the sun. He did look like a god of health and a rebuke to any gainfully employed and responsible human being.

Wenda wants Will to go into writing, I said. She claims Will is ten times the writer Edgar Demming is. Edgar and Wenda were in K-through-six together.

Don't look at me like that, I added. Like I was a stranger or something.

It must have felt odd, standing in his own house after all that time, hearing his children squabbling over toys in the nursery. He seemed like a man who had gone on a long journey to a fabled country where he had had many adventures, only to return and find everything mysteriously the same yet different.

The phone rang again, and I ran to get it.

Yes, this is she, I said. Why, I just got out of the shower, sir, so you can guess what I am wearing. No, sir, I categorically deny that there was any devil worship or demonic possession practised in the church basement, leastways when I was there.

Duffy shook his head and disappeared in the direction of the nursery. I started to blush. So far I was the only one who knew his parents and Wenda and Will and maybe Garnet and Big Raghib were all coming over for dinner that night, that we would all be together. This was a secret that filled me with a vast delight.

This is how it will end, I thought: We're all going to be on Oprah, *People* magazine will send a crew of photographers, *Midnight* will pay us ten thousand dollars each for our stories, and my children will claim to have been fathered by aliens. We are entering a world of fame and fiction. It will turn out that Wallis De Vere is Duffy's Mom's favourite author and that she can somehow forgive Tammy for also being the Whore of Babylon, that Tammy Cudrup and Raghib Natwal will find in each other an unlikely but perfect match, that Duffy has secretly been working on a novel about us all guaranteed to be a bestseller.

The next thing I knew I was huddled in my car next to the palmetto hedge and the basketball hoop I made Will and Garnet install for the twins. Some mysterious force had driven me out there, and I could not tell if I was laughing or crying. The steering wheel gleamed at me like a question mark. The road beyond the paved driveway stretched infinitely in either direction, connecting us with a million other driveways and houses just the same as our own, each harbouring potential or actual novelists and their spouses.

Duffy had always told me to watch the palmettos for rattlers, though I'd never seen one. He seemed haunted by a story he heard when he was a boy about somebody's pet dog running into a nest of rattlers hiding in a palmetto bush. For some reason, I recalled that the Indians used to think the Milky Way was the road west to the Land of the Dead and that somewhere else was another road called the Way of Dogs, which was what dogs used to get to heaven. This made me wonder if there was also a Way of the Rattlesnake and a Way of the Abandoned Housewife.

Presently, Duffy came out and sat with me.

My mom called, he said. She wanted to know if you were expecting her to bring the cheesecake or her tuna casserole this time.

What did you tell her?

Cheesecake.

I sighed, kept my eyes fixed beyond the window, pretending to scan the palmettos for dog-killing reptiles. I could hear the phone ringing and ringing inside. When it stopped, I knew Rachel had answered.

Was that the wrong thing to say? Duffy asked.

We could hear Rachel's voice through the screen door. My name is Rachel, she said, her tone rising with irritation and contempt. Rachel, I said. Rachel. Rachel. Rachel. It's Rachel, butthead. She slammed the phone into its cradle.

4

I KNOW NOW that Duffy is never coming back, also that there is something Biblical in this. Wenda says all men want to be the Prodigal Son and if Duffy's Dad had mentioned that parable one more time that night she would have thrown up.

Tammy Cudrup, looking slightly frumpy in a sweater she borrowed from my dresser drawer to hide her breasts, charmed everyone with her eager smile and shy, trembly voice. You could tell when Tammy said something because someone else would have to shout I beg your pardon and lean across the table. She got Big Raghib to drop his tie in the gravy boat twice. Duffy's mom beamed as if she were about to explode with happiness. And the children were so excited they asked to be excused before they sat down and spent the meal crawling beneath the table guessing what feet belonged to which person.

These are Nannie's.

These are Grampy's.

These are Daddy's.

These are Uncle Will's.

These are Doctor Doctor's.

These are the girl Mommy let sleep all day without getting mad at her.

Every time they mentioned their daddy, they burst into giggles. They were used to seeing him weekend afternoons and for dinner in town now and then, but to have him in their own house, sitting at the table, made them excited and nervous beyond bearing.

Half-way through the meal Duffy pushed his chair back and excused himself and stepped out onto the porch for a cigarette. He had said nothing the whole time. His silence, though genial, cut against the grain of jubilant expectation.

I followed him and we stood there a while, not saying anything because I knew what he was going to say and he knew that I knew what he was going to say — the fact that we said nothing and decided everything has always irritated some members of the family, namely Will, who says you can't make a scene out of silence.

I loved the smell of him then, the slightly frayed, sweaty smell of his clothes, his strong blue tobacco smoke, his deodorant, his breath. And I know the sight of me so close and the sound of the children's voices must have pierced him like a blade.

I slipped my arm around him, intending an affectionate hug, but it turned into something else. He bent down and kissed me and we clung to each other like tired, desperate swimmers, and I thought, oh my, Jethron Ord had nothing on this. We were new people altogether, it seemed, with deeper, more knowing passions. It gave me a dusky thrill like I was cheating. I wanted to drag him down on the runner and peel my panties off, but I didn't only for fear of the children running out.

Afterward we sat on the glider holding hands, abashed, a still-young couple showing inordinate interest in their basketball hoop.

We talk like this now — easy, bantering. And beneath the surface demeanour is a kind of knowing sadness. Neither of us dwell on might-have-beens, but there are avenues of dream no longer open to us.

I was right about one thing though — Tammy Cudrup went after Big Raghib like a heat-seeking missile. She has moved into his house on the bluff overlooking the Gulf and drives his second car, the little Mercedes ragtop, around town. He says it surprised him, but he is convinced she is a good and simple soul with a streak of natural piety that makes her almost Hindu.

Wenda says all unmarried women become Hindu when they turn thirty-five, and did I know Tammy just had a birthday? Wenda talks bitterly like this because she is jealous and because Will went on a trip to L.A. with Edgar Demming to meet producers. What happened over the next week is unclear — Will maintains he slipped on wet tiles in a men's room, knocked his head against a sink and can't remember a thing. But his Visa card bill showed eight thousand dollars in new charges, and he has been receiving phone calls from a woman who works as a publicist for a pornographic film maker.

Duffy is writing a novel called *The Left Ladies Club*, which I am partial to because I am in it. I am the pretty Christian choir girl who falls for a boy named Buffy, a Nietzsche-quoting, Harley-riding high school rebel with a book of Keats and a sawed-off .410 in his saddlebag. Their romance flames up like a gasoline bomb (I quote from the text), then ends abruptly when I catch him in the arms of a bad blond cheerleader.

A year later I read in the paper that he has died in a New Orleans knife fight defending a little black girl from rape. The repentant cheerleader meets me after choir practice one night and tells how, before he died, Buffy left a sample in my name at a sperm bank up on Lake Pontchartrain. The novel ends with two teenagers, a boy and a girl, wading in the Gulf at sunset. They are handsome, wild-haired creatures. They both have tattoos, the word DAD stitched above their hearts. Up the beach, their middle-aged but still beautiful mother watches, shading her eyes with her hand, looking strong and alone.

But I was wrong about this book's chances of turning into a

bestseller. Edgar Demming's agent has turned down eight drafts of the first fifty pages. What Wenda says is that Duffy has remained true to his calling and not sold out to success. He even turned down a job teaching writing at the community college up in Vancleave, preferring to stick with his outdoor work because of the free time it gives him to think and write.

He never said he was sorry, which was a relief. I didn't want the father of my children to be the kind of man who went around saying he was sorry for the messes he created just by being himself. There is altogether too much apologizing going on these days and not enough men and women who drop everything to seek their heart's desire.

He spends evenings and weekends with me and the twins. We have become that new American thing, the sprawling family with exes, almosts and unrelated-but-interested parties replacing the grandparents, aunts, uncles and cousins of the old set-up. I do believe that, with a good heart, we can make the new system work as well as or better than the old.

We do barbecue and potluck on Sunday afternoons, when the air is raucous with laughter and smells of smoked mullet, charred steak and boiled cabbage. Children and dogs tangle underfoot in bumptious chaos. Big Raghib performs string tricks for his new baby, while Tammy and the rest of the Ragged Point literary crowd huddle together over cigarettes and beer, griping about editors and agents and telling dirty jokes. Duffy's dad rubs his knuckles through his crewcut, recites an ecumenical grace he adapted from the Upanishads and hands out HAPPY TOGETHER bumper stickers.

I wish my mother could see us all. We are not at the end of the story, but we have reached a pause in the action. Our voices recede into a sunlit space. We peer into the past with mild astonishment, the future with diffidence and hope. I think how Heaven must be an eternity of moments like this. I think how the Bible teaches that all life is a book and a prayer.

Bad News of the Heart

REC'D DISCHARGE FROM BELLEVUE. Discharge nurse, named Iris McVity, escorted me to public entrance and said I would be a hunk if I had a brain more than a minute and kept off the sauce. So naturally I hung around till she got off work, and we went for a drink in an Irish karaoke bar around the corner. But I could see right away we were a match for the way she smiled when she saw me, a little exasperated but flattered nonetheless, with a sad, knowing glint in her eye.

She was a big girl, maybe forty-five years old, slow yet graceful of movement, with hams like oaks and breasts like small hills, and maybe she hadn't been lucky in the men she had met till now. Something made her think it worthwhile taking a chance on a former patient, fresh from the ward where my friends called me Freud on account of my reading up on the subject at every opportunity. (They also called me Dutch or the Cleaner for other reasons later to be explained.)

We drank three beers and I sang her "The Rose of Tralee" in my uneducated baritone, reading the words from the screen, and she invited me home for bacon and eggs if I promised not to exhibit any symptoms, and I said yes and hefted my book duffel onto my shoulder. There was romance in the air, it was a tonic to both of us. And I thought also that I might, after all, be able to get by without my medication, which I casually sold to a bar patron in the men's room on my way to the street.

It was cold in the night outside, moonless and black like someone had shut the refrigerator door, but we walked arm in arm to the bus stop and hung on straps, nudging each other pleasantly as the bus slithered through the streets. Only one or two strangers seemed suspicious to me, possible android impostors, agents of a foreign power or Central American refugees. I was about to accost a tow-headed waif with the sniffles and a metal ring coming out of her nose (primitive receiving device), when Iris caught my eye with one of her disapproving looks.

She's read my file, I thought. Thinks she knows me through and through, all my secrets. I smiled and, with but a glance in the direction of the waif, demonstrated that I had as much self-control and judgment as the next man.

It had not yet occurred to me that Iris McVity herself might be a cunningly devised machine or a Russian spy. I had started calling her Doschka in the bar, a pet-name she affected to despise. She was large. Many Slavic women are large, great mountainous women with faces like pumpkins and noses like buttons. It should have been a clue, along with the way she had followed me from the hospital and insinuated herself into the fabric of my life.

Doschka, Doschka, I whispered.

Don't call me that, she said. It's not my name.

She lived in a one-room efficiency decorated with a vast collection of paint-by-number horse pictures she had executed herself in her spare time. Stacks of romance novels huddled next to the unmade bed, with drink and dust rings on the topmost covers. Curled, unframed photographs of her parents dangled from bits of tape along the walls. There were no curtains on the single window

overlooking a back court where a lone dog rummaged in upturned
garbage pails and dirty snow.

Everywhere there was an air of disuse, decay, decrepitude and
dust, as if she barely lived there or as if words beginning with the
letter *d* had taken over her life. But she smiled as she bustled about,
turning on lamps, unplugging the carpet sweeper and stowing it
with some difficulty under the bed. She was still wearing her long
coat and seemed breathless from the exertion. Then she disappeared
into the bathroom, and I listened to her pee voluminously as I
dropped my coat and duffel in a closet full of empty paint-by-
number boxes and dirty laundry.

I was just going through the top drawer of her dresser when she
emerged, blowing her bangs up with a hearty sigh, her face fresh
and damp after a wash, her coat looking like a body crouched
behind the toilet.

Doschka, I said.

The doorbell rang. Another young woman tottered in — energetic, irritable, trailing a cloud of cigarette smoke through which
Doschka followed, looking suddenly lost and ineffectual. She had a
pale, liverish complexion and hip-to-ankle braces on both legs. She
stopped when she saw me, aimed her cigarette, and said, Who's he?
Jesus, where do you find these guys?

I said nothing. She was not addressing me. My sweet Slavic
princess, my precious dumpling, seemed suddenly deflated, seemed
far too small for her clothes. She blushed. His name is Hugo, she
said.

The radiators were tapping up a thunder, heat rising, steam
dripping off the windows, winter outside looking more and more
inimical to human life. I was a bit tense. I could manage a simple
two-person dialogue most of the time, provided there was adequate
medical support at hand in case of trouble. But with a third added
to the mix, not to mention my sudden suspicion that, besides me,
unnumbered other men crowded Doschka's life (which made the

situation positively claustrophobic), I felt my hold on reality beginning to falter.

What I had gathered, reading my way through the hospital library, was that the essential structure of human experience is paranoid. The opposition between self and other which defines so-called normal life also defines the paranoid. It's not us against them, it's me against them, and them is everyone else. The self is an oppositional construct, created in a krieg (war) with others — everyone else, women, small dogs, illegal aliens. The essence of becoming is that someone is out to get you. I remembered trying to explain this — oh, on dozens of occasions — to Dr. Gutfreund, who told me my attempts to apply reason and system to human relations were evidence of a deep psychosis.

Doschka was explaining to Vi (this was her name, short for Vidalia, Vitality or Vibrator, I was not sure which) who I was in words and syntax which recalled the insidious bureaucratic efficiency of an intake sheet. Name: Hugo Tangent; Age: 62; Place of Birth: Netherlands; Nationality: Dutch/Resident Alien; Marital Status: Separated; Next of Kin: Jack Vance, son-in-law; Occupation: Cleaner; Diagnosis: Mild schizophrenia, Obsessive Compulsive Disorder, Post Traumatic Stress Syndrome, Cranial Bumps, Irritable Bladder, Nail Biting, Drug and Alcohol Dependency. Upon my admission, she said, someone had signed a Do Not Resuscitate order, which was always kept at the top of my file, though no one could make out the signature.

I listened, with some ambivalence, as she went through my particulars. None of this seemed familiar to me — even my name — though I began right away to feel like I had to pee, and I started to fidget, picking lint off my pants, straightening the pictures I could reach. Doschka glanced at me reprovingly, as if to remind me of my promise, and I stopped. I regretted now selling my medication in the bar, for it occurred to me that I might actually like the medication.

I looked at my hands. Did these look like the hands of a sixty-two-year-old? Yes. Who was I? What was I doing there? Besides the everyday, garden-variety human desires for the love of a large woman and a cheap roof overhead. Who had signed the Do Not Resuscitate order (commonly referred to by those in the medical profession as DNR)? If I had a son-in-law (a prime suspect in the DNR mystery), then I must have a daughter. And a wife! I felt the clammy hand of fate or history upon my shoulder, suddenly felt the whole authoritative weight of selfhood (as defined by a large set of relationships I didn't know I had with people I had never heard of who plainly hated me and wanted me dead).

Vi eyed me suspiciously. I gathered from internal evidence that she was also a nurse, also lived in the building, collected Hummel figurines and glass globe shake-ups, had a brother named Beldon, a mother named Phonita, an ex-lover named Gary, wanted to have a baby by artificial insemination but was afraid she was too old, liked to fantasize about black men, went to Bingo every Friday night with Doschka (whom she insisted on calling Iris), and it was Friday night.

Trying to be friendly, I said I knew Vi's brother Beldon. I'd met him in Nam when he was a gunnery sergeant in a little place called Nop Lop outside of Da Nang where I went to refit after a long range reconnaissance patrol over the DMZ in '63. I sold him eight of the little VC heads I'd brought back in my grenade pouch. Had Vi ever seen any of those heads? I asked.

No, she said, frostily. Beldon was never in Vietnam.

I'd check on that if I were you, I said.

. . .

What about the bacon and eggs? I said to Doschka.

Things were not going well. It was the eternal triangle: recently released mental patient, woman and other woman from down the hall. I didn't know what exactly I'd fallen into, maybe one of those lesbian hookups, or maybe just lonely single ladies with a Bingo lust. But I was in the way. Doschka clearly wanted me there, though she was embarrassed a) by me and b) by having her desires exposed like this in front of her friend. Vi didn't want me there, was jealous of Doschka and didn't like the look of me, though she was also secretly attracted — I have the bad-boy look women love. I felt whipsawed in the violent cross-currents of their desires, a situation bound to make me crazy if I wasn't already and a reminder of why, in the past, my passions had tended to the inanimate.

In session with Dr. Gutfreund, I had once let slip (possibly under the influence of sodium pentathol injections administered surreptitiously) details of my youthful fascination with "lifelike" mechanical toys. What did I mean by lifelike? Gutfreund had demanded. He was always trying to get me to explain myself to myself, which I understand is standard therapeutic technique.

What did I mean by lifelike? I meant moving about, performing complex and repetitive actions up to and including making simple speeches. I loved my little tin drummer boy, a barking dog that turned somersaults when wound up and a frog that hopped. I also loved automated bank tellers, self-serve gas stations and vending machines (there was one in the hospital cafeteria which I took to calling Mother).

Somehow, I told Gutfreund, these machines managed to essentialize all that was good in life while subtracting the emotional confusion and darkness. You never saw a vending machine beat an old woman to death for her handbag, I said. With a machine you know where you stand.

. . .

Which was what I was thinking as we sat down to eat the bacon and eggs. Vi was shaking pepper and cigarette ashes over her eggs. I had my hand on Doschka's knee under the table.

She said, Get your hand off my knee. You said you'd behave.

Doschka, Doschka, I whispered.

She frowned.

I can cook a mean ox tail soup, I said, if you have some spare chicken stock, a bay leaf and an ox.

Vi started to laugh. I liked her laugh. Hell, I was in love with her leg braces (for obvious reasons). My recent sojourn in the ward had taught me that pathology is real. Sometimes it's the only thing you can put your finger on.

We were drinking vodka and powdered fruit juice Vi had brought from her apartment. I'd found some pills in Doschka's top drawer, one of those generic drugs. The name started with "anti" — the rest I couldn't understand — but I thought I'd take some prophylactically.

Vi had warmed to me — her initial defensiveness was typical of women with low self-esteem and physical deformity (all women believe they have low self-esteem and suffer a physical deformity). Once you crack the shell, the real personality starts to come out. Vi was a clown and a flirt, but she was on a clock — no matter how pleasant she got, she had to say something waspish or mean-spirited every five minutes. Doschka was sentimental, romantic and given to witty double entendres. When Vi threw back her head to laugh, Doschka's face would melt into the faintest trace of a smile, enigmatic and lost. The talk turned to sex. Vi told jokes with a hard glitter in her eye; Doschka told stories about former lovers.

It was going as easy as pie, the mood had changed, but for some reason I suddenly grew thoughtful. I looked at the two of them chattering away, glad to have a man to watch them, acting up like schoolgirls, lighting their cigarettes in the candles. Their voices went away from me, the table seemed to lengthen — a hallucinatory sensation not uncommon when I went off the drugs.

I had a moment of peacefulness, when I didn't feel the need to speak, when I could just listen to their cheerful voices. I was the perfect listener. But then just outside that silence I could hear the noisy, hectoring sound of my own voice talking up a storm, trying to make Doschka like me. I hated that voice and I hated Doschka for liking me. I started to speak. I started a story, an old story came out of the silence of the perfect listener, but as soon as I spoke the words they became a bribe, and I got disgusted with myself.

I told them about my sister Luna, the one we always said was the most tangential of the Tangents, how when she was thirteen she began to sleep with German soldiers to help feed our family, how one night she went home with an SS officer who showed her photographs he'd taken in the Death Camps, how they made love that night in a bed littered with pictures of dead Jews, how sweetly and insanely they made love, and how, in the night, the SS officer shot himself to death while Luna held him.

She came home a week later, after being detained for questioning by the authorities. There was an irresistible light in her eyes. She wanted to talk, she told me the whole story — I was a little boy. When she told me how sweetly and insanely they had made love, I didn't know what lovemaking was. She showed me one of the photographs. I started to laugh at the funny naked bodies. She embraced me. Yes, yes, little Hugo, she said. Laugh at the dead. Don't stop laughing. That was my reaction. Then she went out the door and was gone.

After the war, my father searched the DP camps and Red Cross registries, even the cemeteries. In truth, I don't think he looked very hard, though he seemed to be hunting constantly. He felt guilty that his daughter had become a prostitute, that she had slept with Germans. Part of my father didn't want to find Luna, part of him couldn't live without her. Later he hung himself.

I've been looking for her all my life, I told Vi and Doschka.

Is that why you're crazy? asked Vi, refusing to be won over. Doschka wept silently. I put my hand on her knee, she left it there.

It's just a story, I said. I may have made it up.

I had their attention. Love's entry. But it was a mess. The story had calmed me down, but my machine dreams hovered just off stage. I wanted Doschka to love me. But I'd told her a story instead, a story about my sister who disappeared. The subterfuges of love always end up making love impossible. By telling the story I'd seduced Doschka, just as the SS officer used his Death Camp pictures to seduce Luna. But I'd pushed her farther away as well, she was disappearing, fading from sight, just at the moment I pressed my fingers to her knee.

(I had tried to explain this to Dr. Gutfreund one day during session. The vertigo of experience, or our daily experience of vertigo. I told him love and the self were like two dogs chasing each other around a tree. If they ever connected, they'd try to kill one another. He said, But people manage, Hugo. That's the point. People fall in love, get married, have children, muddle along. I loved Dr. Gutfreund just then for his sweet naïveté, his belief that soul-management could keep the wolves out of the kitchen, the forest out of the heart.)

Then Doschka started to speak, to tell a story. She was staring into the candle flame, tears sliding down her face. The first time she had sex, she said, was with her brother Teddy. Vi gasped and nearly swallowed her cigarette. They became lovers when she was fourteen, secretly, though innocently, without guilt. They were in love, she said. It felt so sweet and natural. In bed, they pleased each other, things she'd never had the courage to do with another man. This lasted four years, until Teddy left for college. That Thanksgiving he borrowed a friend's car to drive home to see Doschka, slammed into a concrete abutment in a rain storm and died. She knew it wouldn't have worked, that they were heading for a guilt-ridden and uncomfortable future — or worse, some sordid disaster. But the way it happened she never got to say goodbye.

Now she tried to find Teddy in every man she met. She gazed at me in the candlelight, measuring me against the ideal Teddy. And I knew, for the time being, I looked just like him.

I was in love with her, though unnerved. I don't normally fall in love except when I skip my medication. Her story made me fall in love just as my story had earned me the right to rest my hand upon her knee. Her horse pictures, her dingy apartment, her size, the fact that she was a nurse and hence a maternal figure (yes, even I can admit she was more maternal than a vending machine) — all these made me want to love her. But her story seduced me.

Why? And what is love? An erotic accident prolonged to disaster. Can I say that? Her story was like a dream. The best stories are like dreams, or are dreams, come out of the silence or out of the page like a dream of words. She was lawless and educated in loss. Just the sort of woman I am always looking for to redeem me, to stand by me when my relationship with reality falters.

Dr. Gutfreund said I looked for women like this because I had failed to acquire a good inner object. Maybe my mother dropped me on my head when I was wee. Or I bit her nipple while nursing and she whacked me on the face with a rolled up newspaper. (Don't do this, ladies. It only makes the baby desperate. I learned to bite very hard.)

I glared at Vi (short for Viper, Vicious or Vicuna?), suddenly finding her presence at best a distraction, at worst a pit of evil. I wanted to get a screwdriver and take her apart bolt by bolt. I glanced at Doschka, she was eyeing Vi nervously. Perhaps she was nervous about her friend's reaction to her confession, but it could easily have been a look of love. You can't tell with looks.

Once upon a time, I said — and they both turned to me, slightly irritated — once upon a time, there was a girl named Ghislaine and a boy named Adhemar. They fell in love one day when Ghislaine happened to spy Adhemar and some other boys swimming in a canal naked. Adhemar happened to look up just as Ghislaine saw him, poised for a dive from the tow-path. Ghislaine's eyes met Adhemar's. She blushed and turned coquettishly away, then ran home laughing. Her look, her blush and her flight — the ancient signature of Eros — kindled passion in Adhemar's heart. He slipped on his clothes and followed her to her house, watched her disappear behind the blue door with just one glance back to make sure that he was there.

Who could resist the drama of love and pursuit? Ghislaine and Adhemar were married. But almost as soon as they married, they began to grow bored with one another. Ghislaine invented erotic games to excite them — she flirted with other men, she demanded more money and beautiful things from the already pressed Adhemar. The mood of their marriage developed drastic swings, from lust to contempt. In short order, because they were also dutiful souls, they had two children: a girl, Luna, and a boy named Hugo. This made things worse because Ghislaine no longer felt as if she could run away, and Adhemar, seeing that she was trapped, began to disregard her. For both, this was a tragedy because they could still remember the sweetness of their early love.

The war came, their circumstances grew more difficult. Life for Adhemar and Ghislaine was a treadmill of drudgery and despair. Sometimes Adhemar would try to smile and put his arm around his wife — for the sake of comradeship, for old love. But she had grown spiteful and bitter. And when their daughter disappeared, Ghislaine used the awful event as an excuse to slip away herself into madness.

Exhausted by life, Adhemar yet forced himself to resurrect a ghastly parody of the old game of desire and pursuit, hunting his daughter ceaselessly after the war, though he never found her, perhaps never really wanted to find her because he was afraid of what he would find. At length, having given too much of himself for love, he hung what was left from a beam in the attic where the boy Hugo found him at peace at last.

Vi (short for Viable, Vitamin or Virus?) sighed. She had her hand over her mouth, her eyes were shiny, sad and wide. Doschka looked the same. They could have been twins or a metaphor.

This is what madmen, poets and lovers have in common, the gift of metaphor, the knack of seeing the same in difference. It's what makes life so confusing — you think you're talking to a genius and he turns out to be a dustbin schizophrenic. Or that luminous woman you fell in love with for her wit turns out to have boundary problems. She can't tell the difference between herself and the rest of the world. Metaphor. I had a dream once, that I'd found Luna and died. What does that mean?

There was weeping and gnashing of teeth in the room. I'd taken the girls to a place, very low. We had intensity, often mistaken for love, maybe it was love. The candles were burning low. With a sniff and a scrape at her nose, Doschka got up and began foraging in drawers for more candles. Vi disappeared down the hall for cigarettes and music. I took Doschka in my arms. Her eyes were closed. She kissed me tenderly. What was she seeing? Whose face?

She'll be back, she said. It made it more exciting. She kissed me again. Are you really crazy? she asked. A little voice. Not the nurse who would know the answer, but the lonely dreamer, the meta-phorist, who wanted a different answer.

I was, briefly, sane and said yes. I felt good about myself. I'd told the truth. But it didn't help. Doschka had gone crazy herself.

She said, Well, I don't believe you. I don't want to believe you. I want this to go on and on.

It is my belief that we were very drunk. Vi came limping back with another jug of vodka and more of that powdered juice. She had found a package of drink umbrellas to liven up the party. She had a CD player, put on something bluesy and surprising. The woman had hidden depths, obscure tastes. She began dancing dreamily with her eyes closed, smiling to herself, oddly graceful despite the stringiness of her figure and those leg braces. Doschka was having a candle fugue, maybe twenty glowed around the darkened efficiency, on plates, saucers, upturn coffee mugs. If you squinted, it looked like you were in a church.

I felt sane, though it crossed my mind that I only felt sane because everything around me was insane and intense and some-how reflected what was in my mind. But I wasn't afraid just then. Not at all. Thoughts of androids and double agents seemed far away (yet still there, hovering in mid-distance — once I slept with three women in a row who turned out to be holographic images of women and not real women at all).

Vi beckoned me with a lit cigarette and a worldly look. We began to dance, our bodies aligned, folded together from knee to temple. She blew smoke in my ear. I caught sight of Doschka, half in shadow like the moon, watching us with a forlorn expression on her face. Keep this up, I said to myself, and you'll be back in the jug in a week.

Vi stroked the nape of my neck and said, Shh. I hadn't been

speaking, but I knew what she meant. I had stuck two of the drink umbrellas behind my ears — she lifted them out and dropped them on the floor. She whispered, I'm in love with Iris. That's my story. Look at her. She knows that I'm telling you. We've been together for ages, but it's always like this. When I make love to her, she shuts her eyes. She says, yes, yes, and lets herself go but never looks at me. She pretends it's not happening. But while she's pretending it's not happening, she can do anything.

That's not all. Once, when we were just together, she had an affair. She's like that. She gets sad and men notice and take advantage. When she's sad she thinks she needs them. When she told me, the bottom fell out. I cried and cried as if the world had ended. Iris was kind. She held me, let me rage, fed me orange slices and sips of vodka in an egg cup, read me a love letter I'd written her, her soft voice saying my words of love in the darkness.

I should have left her. Instead my desire changed. Instead of wanting to make love to Iris, I wanted Iris to make love with men while I watched or listened in the next room or waited outside. I wanted her to come to me after, soaked with sweat, smelling of man, blowsy and relaxed from pleasure, and hold me and tell me what she had done and whisper that she loved me. In the moment when she betrayed me, I had lost Iris forever. But she taught me to love the pain, and I when I make love now it is not to a woman named Iris but to a woman who is never there, who is always betraying me. My desire has become impure. I'm a sick fuck. All for love. Even if she were to leave me, I would still want love like that. The only way I can get out of this is to kill myself.

Her voice had gone gravelly and strained. The hair went up the back of my neck at her final words. Poor Vi. One thing to lose a lover, another to lose the ability to love. Never such loneliness in a voice (other than my own sometimes). I tried to push away, but she held me fiercely.

Despite myself, I was getting aroused. First Doschka, now this. It's not my name, I heard her say. Yes, I thought, with a sickening drop in my gut, you're always mistaking this one or that one for someone else. Reality is tangled. They tell you there's a path, but all of a sudden there are eighty-nine paths or none at all. In any situation, you think you're in charge, only to find out the situation is in charge of you.

I have tried to explain this sensation to Dr. Gutfreund — the moment when you'd rather be a chair or a rock or dead because you're tired of tap dancing in the strobe light. Gutfreund always said, somewhat impenetrably, You feel like that, Hugo, because you're crazy. Take your pills. He said this in a kind way. I always liked talking to him, though I tended to exaggerate, put him on, give him the juice. Sometimes he would get it and laugh.

I was trapped between Vi and Doschka (all right, Iris — even I was beginning to see past my own pathology to her pathology — Iris was its name, and she looked Dutch, not Slavic). I was no longer myself but a figure in their erotic tableau, the necessary accelerant for the firestorm (metaphor) of their love. As the evening wore on, I had been feeling distinctly seedy. Low self-esteem and all that. As if I were disappearing inside my clothes. And as I disappeared I became more and more anxious, fidgety, full of desire — for what? Call it love, but it could have been anything intense, explosive. Fill me up, I thought, just fill me up with light. Then turn out the light.

But even I could see there was something the teensiest bit unhealthy about this. I needed a delay, time to think.

Candles all around, the two werewolf women, melancholy with their desires, giving me the eye, horses everywhere I looked, some of them with the little numbers showing through the paint; it seemed utterly dark and human, a story of love, bad news of the heart. And I knew I was going to be the one to go back to the ward for this because inside the machine called Hugo Tangent there was an ON/OFF switch which went click when things got too painful or confusing. I wasn't worried about this — I was just waiting for the click.

But I started to speak, nothing fancy, just another story.

Once upon a time there was a boy named Hugo who liked to clean. After he found his father like that, he cleaned the house, then he went out and began to clean the street. He went into the neighbours' houses and cleaned them. He used small brushes, buffing cloths and little pans of soapy water because he was very thorough.

This was in Holland, which is a very clean country. At first people didn't mind, especially after the war when things were such a mess. The country was having a national cleaning frenzy anyway. But soon the neighbours began to get nervous. One day he almost cleaned Mrs. Eindorp's cat Millie to death. Mr. Oostijen, two doors down, nearly ran over Hugo with his Renault when he didn't notice the boy beneath the car cleaning the undercarriage. The boy cleaned all the blossoms off Mrs. Henke's prize-winning tulips. One morning Hugo was found at the canal at the foot of the street cleaning the water. He wasn't eating, no one was taking care of him. He talked only to a collection of wind-up toys he carried in his crazy mother's net grocery bag. So Hugo was packed off to a hospital for children who cleaned too much and had no family. The hospital was crowded already. It was a very clean hospital.

A few years later, one of the hospital nurses (hefty Dutch girl, big thighs) told Hugo that he ought to go to America to look for his sister. Lots of DPs went to America, she said, to escape the past and start fresh. When she told him this, the nurse and Hugo were making love in a broom closet where Hugo kept his cleaning supplies and wind-up toys.

The nurse was in love with Hugo. Hugo couldn't tell if the nurse was a wind-up toy or a Russian spy. But he listened to her and soon after found his way to New York where he took a day job in a laundry and a night job cleaning offices on Wall Street. Later he opened a string of dry-cleaning stores in the boroughs. Got rich.

Hugo never found Luna, though he took out ads in newspapers and hounded the immigration authorities. Nights he would walk the streets accosting women, repeating her name. Often, when he was making love to a woman, he would be stricken with the thought that it might be Luna herself (and not a wind-up toy).

He was a glutton for sadness and stories. He saw her in the streets a dozen times a night. She would be standing just off the curb in the moonlight, skinny, waifish and blond, with eyes like bruises, with her thumb up or just waiting for whatever darkness came in a car. Scared to death or stoned or strung out. He fell in love with them. He would speak to them softly in Dutch. He would try to save them, though hardly any of them wanted to be saved and most mistook his motives.

They broke his heart over and over, always leaving in the night, going off with his money, coming round with their boyfriends or pimps for more money, telephoning into his sleep from distant call boxes, whispering words of hate and desperate need or love, which was the same thing. It didn't matter. It was what Hugo expected. That kind of love.

One he married — Louella from Tennessee. He met her outside a cemetery one night, turning tricks in a crypt. She had white-blond hair in spikes, cheeks like a skull. She was already pregnant. It made her want to be good. She was certain she loved him. She had Luna's eyes. She was certain it wouldn't work. He tried to protect her, make her feel safe. She got bored, she hated him. After the baby came, she left, telephoning from call boxes in a dozen states, getting fainter and fainter. How's my baby? Tell her I love her. He called the baby Moon.

When Moon was five, Louella swept back like a malign wind out of the West. She had gone to prison, found Jesus, hated men. She came to the door with two cops, a social worker, and a court order to rescue Moon. I have to put my life back together, she told Hugo.

She looked twenty years older. The muscles in her cheeks jumped with rage. Moon was screaming, Daddy! Daddy! The only thing he could think to do was lie and tell her he would follow shortly, that they would never be apart again. He packed her an overnight bag with her favourite dolls and wind-up toys. It was like packing a tiny coffin with the belongings of the dead. He did not know what Hell she was going to. He kissed her goodbye on the forehead, on her lips, on her fingers. She was sobbing quietly in the social worker's arms. She believed him.

Hugo thought, What a strange little wind-up toy that woman is carrying. It seems so lifelike, with eyes just like my sister's. And then he thought, We are being destroyed by love.

Hugo woke up in a hospital with a mop in his hand, speaking to a water fountain. He still remembers the water fountain fondly, though they are no longer in touch. Then he was in and out of hospitals. When he was out, Louella appeared asking for support for Moon, asking for money for psychiatrists to repair the damage he'd done to their daughter. She said, You'll never get rid of me. Hugo thought, This is funny. I can't find my sister. I've lost my daughter. But I've got an alien for a wife who's sunk a tether into my heart.

Once Louella had him arrested for molesting Moon. Hugo was hopeful. He thought he might get to see Moon if she testified in court. But then he was in a hospital again, the charges dropped. Louella kept saying Jack this and Jack that. Hugo thought Jack was her boyfriend, but then Jack married Moon back in Memphis. She was fifteen. Louella asked Hugo to pay for the wedding. You can't come, she said. She hates you. Jack wants to kill you after what you did.

Louella looked like death, looked exactly how Hugo thought Luna would look, given the life she led. She was on something, cranked up, every time he saw her, breathless with the excitement of confrontation. She made him want to kill himself. When it got intense like that, he would think, This is love. This is what love is all about.

Once, in remission from his lunacy, he was staring out his apartment window. He heard muffled thuds, the crash of glass breaking somewhere above. Then a shape flashed in front of him, pink and white with handles in the back. Wheelbarrow, he thought. Or a doll. After, as he watched the crowd gather below, he realized it had been a woman jumping to her death. What sadness had driven her to this desperate act Hugo could not tell. Though he read in the papers how she had run away from a husband who beat her, lived in shelters and half-way houses and lost her child to the Department of Social Services.

Sometimes, now, the skies seemed full of falling women, thin blond Dutch girls with their eyes wide open, mouths gaping in voiceless screams, legs out like the handles of a wheelbarrow.

Vi and Iris were holding hands across the table, their eyes fixed on a candle flame. They seemed still to be listening like lost children to the words of an old story. I could feel the click coming like a blessing, like the hand of God or like the doctor's hand closing the eyes of the dead, which, though unseeing, seem to stare greedily, to be unwilling to let go the terrible, fleeting incandescence of the world.

Fill me up with light, I thought again. I prayed. And turn out the light.

I remembered Mama in her madness reading from the Book of Revelation, the sombre, awful, insistent repetitions of the call: Come, come, Lord Jesus. Even so, Come.

Yes, yes, I thought. Come save me. Save us from this gorgeous world of love, place of torture. I could feel the click coming. This might be the record, I thought. Out of the ward and back inside in about six hours. Long enough to remember what I was always trying not to remember, that the world is a Hell of tortured souls and demons — not machines or aliens or wind-up toys.

I pictured Iris (not Doschka) gently leading me to the taxi, giving the address, then taking me by the hand at the hospital entrance, just as the electric eye picks us up, recognizes me and opens the door in welcome. Perhaps she'll envy me my sweet confusion, that envy being the insanity of the sane who hold themselves steadfastly to the flame even as they yearn for it to end.

Briefly I was myself, someone I hardly knew, only visited from time to time and barely recognized. With a sudden clarity, I thought how clarity itself is a species of redemption, and how this melancholy moment just before the click, when I saw my story — and everyone else's — whole and unendurable, was a moment of equilibrium, of wisdom, tinged ever so slightly with meaning. It was nothing I could hold onto.

The click was coming, I wanted it. Come, come, Lord Jesus. Even so, Come.

Vi and Iris were in that moment, too, part of the universal tragedy. We were companions in arms, which is the most you can hope for. A nod of recognition across the broken ground in the flash of shellfire. Before we go back to killing each other. An extension of the krieg (war) metaphor — something to tell Dr. Gutfreund next session. The self not created in strife but dismantled, shivered, exploded, until the moment when there is no self, when the not-self shimmers like a mirage, like pure yearning, and disappears.

Iris turned to me with gentle eyes, her hospital eyes. She had always been a good nurse, schooled in sadness. I was eating one of

Vi's drink umbrellas, beginning to make circular, scrubbing motions with my hand upon the tabletop. Even so, Come, I thought. I felt like a bug with a pin in my back.

She took me by the hand, Vi took my other hand. Nurses' hands. Kindly and efficient, not so warm, slightly distanced. They led me to the bed and pushed me down. I felt their bodies on either side. I felt a cool hand on my forehead, like Mama's hand, though Mama had never been much of a mother. I felt someone ruffle my hair with her fingers, begin to scratch my scalp ever so gently. It was almost too hot between them, but the heat made me drowsy. I wanted to sleep. I wanted the hand to go on rubbing my head.

I'm going now, I said out loud.

Shh, someone said.

Abrupt Extinctions
at the End of the Cretaceous

WE WERE TIRED.

Yes, it was as simple as that.

Many of us had been around for millions, if not hundreds of millions, of years. No one alive today, save for some of the insect brethren, can conceive of what one friend, a gentle and extremely large herbivore with a brain in his neck, called our flirtation with eternity.

And size.

Yes, our fierce and ingenious assault upon the limits of biomass, our penchant for baroque topological whimsy, our sheer, well-nigh insane inventiveness in nutrient-energy conversion, secondary and tertiary nervous systems, skeletal buttressing and heat conservation/ replacement mechanisms. This was our art, our passion.

For which we made sacrifices.

My friend, the herbivore already mentioned, lived his whole life along the shore of a shallow lagoon, half-submerged so that the water would help support him, take the stress off his knees. By day he would raise his eyes to the distant mountains or the nearer forest verges, pondering their mysteries. By night he would watch the moon in a mood of melancholy wonderment, dreaming of journeys he would never take.

He had to eat continuously — possessing a small head and

mouth atop a long neck, he was obliged to eat steadily day and night with barely a pause here and there for a cat nap. Yet if he slept too long, as likely as not he would fall prey to one of the giant meat-eating predators who themselves were compelled to forage constantly in an endless drama of slaughter, gore and piteous squeals for mercy.

It was, in short, a monstrous Schopenhauerian Hell of pure will, struggle and ambition in which each must needs grow and destroy in order to exist.

Near the end, the last fifty million years or so, we were looking for an excuse. My friend wished only to roll on his side, rest his head on the sand and be at peace. But he knew that once down, he would never get up again. To paraphrase one of your great poets of fatigue, he couldn't go on, but he would go on. We had lost our souls to pride. What, in more recent times, have come to be called "quality of life issues" became paramount.

So that long before that fatal comet offered its final solution to what had become a tawdry slide into decadence and death — how the small ones would laugh as the great ones offered their necks to the slashing teeth — we had begun quietly to turn ourselves off.

My friend was a case in point. For years he had been in love with a female who lived in the next lagoon. In season, he would catch her scent on the breeze and hear the faint, plaintive TO-WOOMP, TO-WOOMP of the throat-bladder drumming peculiar to the female of the species.

Once he had made the arduous journey over a low-lying sand spit, no more than fifty yards across but nearly insurmountable to my friend. They had made love along the shore — a dangerous, ungainly, awkward act that was yet full of a wan sweetness — and then, utterly spent, he had trudged back over the sand spit, for the ecosystem of her lagoon was not large enough to support the two of them.

In due course, a child was born, dropped in the tepid waters near the shore where she might have a chance to stumble to her feet before she drowned. But so ungainly had the young become in those days that she broke her neck on impact and lay there stunned, breathing quietly for half a day before scavenging mammals began to nibble at her still living flanks.

My friend and his lover lived many years after that. Stretching their necks to the uttermost, they could see one another over the sand spit. He could smell her scent and hear the melancholy throat-bladder drumming. But they both knew it was all going-through-the-motions, that no one, least of all my friend, had the heart to respond.

One day they heard the whistling exhalation of a large predator on the hunt — a gigantic, bony beast with patchy, lichen-coloured skin and open sores, monstrous teeth and red, haunted eyes. It was barely alive, yet hunting, hunting endlessly, killing whatever came in its path.

Run! Run! my friend called. Go to the centre of the lagoon, go to the deeper water. But the gentle cow only looked at him sorrowfully and bent her head to crop another mouthful of sedge.

When the end came, it was swift but perhaps not merciful. The predator splashed toward her, ugly, driven, his eyes betraying his own lust for release. She lunged awkwardly, stumbling and collapsing forward on her chest, a position from which she could never rise, and then, in a gesture which was to become more and more common, stretched her neck out along the surface of the murky lagoon and turned her eyes appealingly toward her killer.

My friend lived on alone for eons, it seemed to him, watching the planet go to sleep as one species after another, individual by individual, gave up the struggle. After a time, there were not even enough scavengers to clean up rotting mounds of flesh dotting the shorelines. The sharp, greasy smell of putrefaction filled the atmosphere. The little creatures — brother insect, brother mammal — prospered in the feculent and endless supply of meat.

My friend watched and forgave them their teeming glee. He could dream the future as he dreamed the past and foresaw everything, the rise and fall of cities, civilizations, species, the extinction of the sun, the final infinitely cold inertness of time.

He foresaw the coming of the comet, saw the flash of impact over the horizon, felt the earth shudder, saw the great clouds of dust spread ominously, blotting out the sun, felt the first blast of cold, saw ice rime form over the lagoon, felt the plates of thin ice dangling from his knees as he walked.

He watched the great dying end in a last spasm, and then he himself began to expire. He stopped eating and turned his will-power, the awesome strength of his instincts, against himself. He watched the dim sun set behind his beloved mountains. He felt rather than saw the pearlescent glow of the moon beyond the dust clouds.

Dying, he dreamed of his lover and his own epic yet futile trek over the sand spit. He wondered what it would have been like if his offspring had lived, if he and the gentle cow had somehow been able to find a lagoon big enough to support them all.

He could not say, as so many naive commentators have proposed, that all life is good. It did not seem so to him, and, like all the rest of us, he welcomed death. But as his huge legs shivered and buckled, as the mass of his ancient body collapsed around his lungs and heart and, one by one, his brains shut down, he felt a cold, immense and unquenchable pride in what had been attempted and the awesome failure of his race.

Lunar Sensitivities

I

I WENT TO SEE NORRIS. He keeps to himself too much. It's almost pathological the way he avoids visitors, even his best friends. He screens his phone calls, refuses to answer his mail. There used to be a point to this. Norris was once an expert on North American freshwater bivalves, unusual in this respect: he was not connected with any university or institute. He had a little old money from his grandmother, Ottawa lumber money managed astutely during the Great Depression. So he never worked except at his scientific research, which for years took up easily ten or twelve hours a day. He published one book and a dozen or so papers, but as the years passed he produced less and less. He preserved his habitual work schedule, one barely saw him from one week to the next, but I had the impression that he was standing still, worse than standing still, he was wearing himself out with work that wasn't work any more, just soulless drudgery. It seems odd to suggest that freshwater bivalves might have lost their scientific charm for want of human contact.

When he was younger, Norris had tried to keep up with the outside world. For years, he and I maintained a standing Tuesday night dinner engagement at the Tandoori Indian restaurant located near the west end of St. Catherine Street almost exactly halfway between our homes. Sometimes another friend of his, Kaplovsky, would come along as well. When Kaplovsky was there, he and Norris would end up arguing over a book of chess problems or the latest gene-splicing technology or a New Music concert Kaplovsky had attended. Norris would listen to Kaplovsky's description of the concert and then carry on the conversation as if, in fact, he, Norris, had been there himself. Kaplovsky had a job as a computer programmer in the McGill University biology labs. He worked mostly for government grants and the pittance he got as a research assistant. Norris said Kaplovsky was brilliant but unstable and agoraphobic. He only came to dinner when he was taking his medicine and it was working.

Unlike Norris, Kaplovsky had once been married — to a French-Canadian violinist named Marie-Ève. Kaplovsky never talked about his earlier life, but Norris knew all about it anyway, seemed actually to hold his friend in some awe. "You understand, don't you?" he would say. "Kaplovsky had a life before all this. She was fourteen when they met, a prodigy. Her parents had him up on charges, but he and Marie-Ève ran away to Mexico, got married and lived in Cuernavaca for a year. All that time her parents were working on her, undermining her confidence, begging her to return. One day Kaplovsky came home and found her gone, her beloved violin in pieces on the floor. She had returned to Montreal. He never saw her again — but she calls him now, sends him e-mail messages, letters. She suffered a nervous breakdown after she returned, then a car accident that permanently damaged the fingers of one hand. It's all very tragic."

Norris always seemed regretful when he told me about Kaplovsky's life. I had two distinct impressions: that he regretted not having a romantic past that would somehow humanize his own isolated and super-disciplined existence, and that, strangely enough, in talking about Kaplovsky he was also talking about himself— as if what he said about Kaplovsky had actually happened to him, Norris, and that Kaplovsky, who indeed seemed to have no interest in anything other than chess problems and New Music, was nothing but an occasion for an encoded description of Norris's own secret life.

But, of course, Norris had no secret life, or so I thought until a month ago, when something happened in regard to Norris that took me completely by surprise and, indeed, threatened briefly to upset the tender balance of my entire existence. It happened one morning at about eleven o'clock, when I habitually left my apartment on de Maisonneuve and Fort and walked over to the newspaper store on St. Catherine Street to pick up the four or five international dailies I read. I passed the Tandoori Indian restaurant, which was just opening at that hour for the lunch crowd. I looked through the window and, to my consternation, spied Norris seated at our usual table. (I say "usual," though, in fact, we had long ago dropped our old habit of the Tuesday evening dinners.)

He was sitting across from an extraordinarily pretty young woman, someone perhaps in her late thirties, sad-looking, with large washed-out blue-grey eyes and untidy short blond hair. She wore a glove on her left hand, a long black glove that came up to her elbow, something appropriate for evening wear, I thought. They were both smoking cigarettes, though I had never seen Norris smoking a cigarette in my life. I hadn't actually seen Norris in, what, eight months or a year — yes, our friendship had lapsed as his scientific work occupied him more and more (and became less and less productive). He looked inestimably older than the last time we met, worn out, thinner. And the pencil-line moustache he had always affected, like some Hollywood Lothario of the twenties, had turned completely white.

The phrase "scene of passion" floated into my mind, though the word "passion" was one I never before would have connected with Norris. I noted that he held his cigarette between the third and fourth fingers of his right hand, masking the lower half of his face when he brought it to his lips. Another affectation, it seemed to me. And I was filled with contempt and a sense of betrayal by the very sight of this gesture.

The young woman seemed nervous yet animated. Her face was luminously alive, though I could not for the life of me tell you exactly what that means. While I stood there, staring like a common voyeur through the Tandoori Indian restaurant window, she carefully shook a cigarette out of a pack on the table and placed it between the stiff and resisting fingers of her gloved hand before raising it to her mouth for Norris to light.

I was at once fascinated and revolted by the scene and, of course, terrified that Norris might turn and discover me there. I think also that I was instantaneously certain who the woman was, as if I had known her myself in a previous life. And I was in love with her. Or the image of Norris's obvious desire for her injected into my own soul a parallel desire just as, I am certain now, the story of Kaplovsky's marriage had infected Norris with the virus of love. And I recalled a strange thing Kaplovsky had once said, according to Norris (I was not present at most of their conversations — Norris had, really, two separate friendships which occasionally coincided at the Tandoori Indian restaurant). He said, "My entire life has been a struggle to liberate myself from love."

It seemed nonsensical at the time because if there was ever a man who seemed immune to the lunar compulsions of the opposite sex it was Kaplovsky, unless, of course, one considered Norris, who was impervious. But I recall that Kaplovsky's claim had a surprising effect on Norris. "What does he mean?" Norris kept asking, punctuating each reiteration of the question by violently jabbing the tabletop with his pointer finger. "What does he mean by it?" I had never seen Norris so excited, not even during his frequent confrontations with Kaplovsky over obscure chess problems or the random complexities of New Music. And, of course, I had no answer. But I did recall one other occasion (at which I was present, another of those interminable dinners at the self-same Tandoori Indian restaurant) when, at the height of the Referendum debate then sweeping the city, Kaplovsky sighed deeply and said, apparently apropos of nothing, "We must learn to say goodbye and I love you in the same breath."

Watching Norris through the Tandoori Indian restaurant window (trying also to tear myself away), I was suddenly filled with admiration for Kaplovsky and began to remember all sorts of fugitive remarks of his, some reported to me by the envious Norris, some heard in the heat of battle, as it were, seated at our table in the restaurant over steaming plates of curry. Once, during a particularly fractious interchange over the composer John Cage (whom Norris mistakenly insisted on calling Nicolas Cage, confusing him with a Hollywood actor with the same surname, thus confirming his complete ignorance of anything to do with New Music), Kaplovsky suddenly said, "Clams open up when you apply heat. You're the bivalve expert. You should know this."

Norris turned crimson from the peak of his thinning hair down to the pencil-line of his moustache, beneath which his lips went pale, and he seemed in the grip of a paroxysm of rage which he controlled only with great difficulty. Kaplovsky, on the other hand, seemed relaxed and in good humour. His face wore a strange half-smile, enigmatic yet familiar to me. And I had an intuition then — though it seemed against all my previous understanding and experience — that Kaplovsky was somehow at the centre of Norris's existence, that Norris was mesmerized by Kaplovsky, that he measured every accomplishment, every experience, every thought, every flicker of emotion, against Kaplovsky and found himself wanting.

I sensed this though, in conversation, Norris would always present Kaplovsky as the weaker partner, someone he kept up with more out of pity than for any motive of real friendship. It was always: "You know what's happened to poor Kaplovsky now? We'll have to invite him out again — it's the only social life he has." Or: "Poor Kaplovsky's in the soup again. He mixed up his medication and stopped going to the lab. They called me — can you imagine it? I hardly know the man." Or: "Kaplovsky's a sad case, completely crippled by his fear of open spaces, crowds, tall buildings. Clouds! You know he can't look up. Clouds and stars terrify him."

And, of course, I hardly ever saw Kaplovsky. I can count all the times the computer programmer came to dinner with us on one hand, and this was stretched over the ten or so years Norris and I met Tuesday evenings at the Tandoori Indian restaurant. I only saw Kaplovsky on two other occasions, both times at my apartment, where he appeared unannounced and alone, during what I called the Housekeeper Wars, when Norris relentlessly campaigned to suborn Kaplovsky's housekeeper, in effect hijacked or stole her away from Kaplovsky.

She only worked one afternoon a week for Kaplovsky, she worked for other employers as well. But Norris used his seemingly inexhaustible financial resources to hire her for the full week at a considerable advance in pay, the whole week so that she could not possibly fit Kaplovsky in. This was the famous Angie Gosselin episode. She was young, just starting in the housekeeper business, with unusually small hands and feet and large hips, a tall, healthy girl who had once done folk-dancing on the stage. She could prepare lovely pastas, stir-fries or poached salmon for luncheon and engage in topical conversation while she worked. So that if there was ever anyone Kaplovsky might have fallen in love with (besides Marie-Ève, his wife), Angie Gosselin was she. But Norris stole her, despite the fact that he had lived for years in a smallish two-bedroom apartment sparsely furnished in a functional Bauhaus style dating from his youth, which clearly needed no more than a few hours' dusting now and then.

Both times Kaplovsky appeared on my doorstep he was pale, sweaty, clearly under stress, but otherwise his usual courtly self. Both times he brought a book of chess problems that he offered as an excuse. "I knew you would be interested in this intriguing situation," he said, holding the book open, and I was not certain which situation he was talking about, the chess problem or

Kaplovsky's situation with Norris in regard to Angie Gosselin. Indeed, it became clear as each meeting progressed that Kaplovsky was talking about Norris and Angie while trying desperately not to, as though, in fact, he missed Norris, perhaps missed Norris more than he missed Angie Gosselin. And yet there was something almost heroic about the grace, the tact, the extreme courtesy which Kaplovsky exhibited in circumstances so revealing, so highly charged, so potentially embarrassing. After all, these were two scientific professionals, old friends, acting out some intimate and primitive drama over a woman who, to any outside observer, was nothing more than a housekeeper. That she was not simply a housekeeper did not become clear to me until later.

At first, I could only watch and pity poor Kaplovsky for the obvious terror he manifested and overcame every time he went out of doors, the struggle he went through to seek human contact, which contact was at the same time utterly abhorrent if not to say completely horrifying to him. He told me the second time he visited that he could not take the elevator in my building, though my apartment was on the fourteenth floor. Standing in my doorway, holding up his pathetic little book of chess problems, Kaplovsky could never resist a terrified peek over his shoulder, as if his demons might materialize at any moment out of the empty air behind him. Each time he left my apartment he would, with some embarrassment, edge sideways down the corridor with his back to the wall, pause at the elevator door as if trying to summon the courage to enter, then give up and edge towards the stairwell, nodding slightly as he disappeared.

On each of his visits, I made him a lunch — sesame seed cakes, orange slices and Chartreuse in little glasses — which he barely ate but which I could see deeply touched him. And I recalled how at the Tandoori Indian restaurant I had never seen Kaplovsky take a bite of the food he ordered. Indeed, it often happened that Norris would eat as much from Kaplovsky's plate as he would from his own, partly because Kaplovsky was the more adventurous gourmand, always ordering some obscure delicacy, often something not on the menu at all but which he was familiar with through his extensive travels in India (when had Kaplovsky been to India?). Norris would be irritated, would have to taste what Kaplovsky had ordered and then, while complaining about it, eat the entire meal as well as his own. Kaplovsky never seemed to mind, he seemed to live on air and talk and argument.

The Angie Gosselin episode put an end to our Tuesday night dinners. Norris and I never met again at the Tandoori Indian restaurant. I met him occasionally at other venues — he preferred a small, cheap Salvadorean restaurant called La Carreta on St. Zotique, a place he had discovered through Angie Gosselin. But our relationship was never the same, and I must confess that here I was partly to blame, for, following Kaplovsky's second visit to my apartment, I took the extreme action of walking to Norris's apartment building and ringing his doorbell. This was not the first time I had visited Norris, but I was not a frequent guest in his home. This time my visit was in the nature of an invasion.

I was, after seeing poor Kaplovsky in extremis, somewhat hot. I did not feel Norris had treated our friend fairly. I had heard but always discounted rumours that some of the ideas for Norris's papers on bivalves had come from Kaplovsky, who once dabbled himself in bivalve studies, who had indeed once written a paper on the influence of the moon on an obscure and nearly extinct subspecies of mollusc found mainly in Long Point Bay on the north shore of Lake Erie. Norris told me about this paper, scoffing at its amateurish research, its poor statistical analysis, its paucity of raw data (he claimed that in fact the mollusc may already have become extinct or may never have existed, may have been a figment of Kaplovsky's fevered imagination). Kaplovsky's paper had been rejected by all the journals.

"When was Kaplovsky ever at Long Point Bay?" I had asked, somewhat irritated at the way this man Kaplovsky, so reclusive and timid, seemed also to have been everywhere and done everything. (I have not mentioned my own investigations into bivalve arcana, which, compared to those of my two friends, were strictly amateurish and of private interest only — although I expended the better part of a small personal fortune, spent years in the field, in my efforts to achieve some morsel of bibliographic immortality.) And I recalled something Kaplovsky said to me during his first visit to my apartment: "You feel as if someone is stalking you, but when you look, there's no one there. Then suddenly the monster materializes across the table from you."

I had not understood what he meant until I faced Norris, who was unshaven, haggard, almost demented-looking, much worse off than Kaplovsky, it seemed. He was still wearing his pyjamas, though it was mid-morning, a breach of etiquette I would never have expected in a man so correct and dignified. I could see he did not want to let me in; there was a war going on behind his eyes. I had the distinct feeling that Norris was in the grip of a compulsion, or that there were two Norrises struggling for supremacy. But the demands of friendship and a desire not to appear completely overwrought (much the same as Kaplovsky's own forced gallantry when he appeared at my apartment) won out.

We sat in the dining nook at the austere little table where Norris often worked, which indeed was stacked with his notebooks, manuscripts, journals, computer print-outs and reference texts both ancient and modern, and I had just begun to remonstrate with him when, to my horror and amazement, a person I could only assume was none other than Angie Gosselin herself appeared, slipping in from the bedroom wearing Norris's dark green bathrobe, a sleepy look in her eye. Unsummoned, the phrase "transformed by guilt" floated into my mind.

Norris himself could not look at me, but when she stood beside him and placed her small hand upon his shoulder, he sighed a sigh that was almost a moan, almost a cry of pleasure. And his lips seemed to shape themselves into the ghost of a smile, an enigmatic grimace of triumph which at the same time expressed utter despair.

I, who had never set eyes on Angie Gosselin, who had heard only reports of her extraordinary beauty and allure, was instantaneously in love with her, could understand in a flash Kaplovsky's loss, Norris's obsession. I rose from my seat, knocking the chair over in my haste, and, muttering apologies for my intrusion, hurried away. Norris did not get up, failed even to raise his eyes to see me go, only lifted one hand almost languidly to acknowledge my departure.

It was now that Norris commenced work on his last and greatest paper, his famous "Lunar Sensitivities in Certain Great Lakes Subspecies," in which he proved decisively that a sequence of hormonal changes occurs in a rare littoral mussel through the phases of the moon, which mussel indeed apparently moves with the moon, a slow, legless dance to unheard music, an adagio perhaps, which Norris described in his conclusion as the stately back beat of existence, a rhythm of life which might yet be demonstrated to govern us all.

What was most praised in this paper, what gave it an aesthetic as well as a scientific dimension, were the superb drawings, sketches of the patterns carved in the sand by the peregrinations of these strange mussels, amazing natural hieroglyphs, maps of the soul, Norris called them. These drawings were made by none other than Angie Gosselin, who had copied them from Kaplovsky's notes while she was his housekeeper, a fact which she communicated to me some months later when, yes, she became my housekeeper.

I cannot say that I acted well in this, that I was any better than Norris, who had conducted his own relentless and unfair campaign to seduce Angie Gosselin from our friend Kaplovsky. And much later — the moment outside the Tandoori Indian restaurant when I saw Norris with the unhappy young woman and her elegant glove — I was able to see how all this prefigured and foreshadowed events to come, just as the present situation echoed and reiterated previous events; that we are ruled by a kind of repetition, or as Norris himself (following Kaplovsky's earlier, unpublished intuitions) wrote in "Lunar Sensitivities," by obscure and incomprehensible motivations which appear alien and random but are in fact the results of motion fused with form; that motion fused with form is a definition of life itself.

It was a mad, bleak vision — life as an utterly meaningless dance — which was finally Kaplovsky's vision, not Norris's. This is what I think, at least, that Norris was always a nineteenth century man, a Romantic, if you will, while Kaplovsky was firmly based in the late twentieth century, that his agoraphobia was nothing more nor less than the spirit of the age.

And I was thinking all this that day, not very long ago, when I set out to visit Norris finally, after years of seeing him at infrequent and ever more lengthy intervals, years of separation, as it were, bitterness, recrimination, guilt and ennui (yes, it took years to get over the Housekeeper Wars, the Angie Gosselin episode). And perhaps I would never have gone to visit him had I not stopped and peeped in the window of the Tandoori Indian restaurant and seen Norris smoking a cigarette with a woman who was undoubtedly Marie-Ève.

I had not seen Kaplovsky since his second visit to my apartment. I had heard of him infrequently from Norris, who could not resist gossiping about his poor friend during our rare, stiff and anxious meals at La Carreta on St. Zotique. Indeed, it seemed sometimes as if Kaplovsky was all he could talk about, as if every other topic was, for us, taboo. But all the news was bad, only sad tales of Kaplovsky's disintegrating mental processes, his decline into poverty, infirmity and depression. In the last years, he had begun to keep cats, Norris said, a disgusting house pet in his opinion, although he himself had recently been forced to take in a one-eyed, diseased stray which had cost him endless visits to the vet and many sleepless nights of care.

I had not seen Norris, as I say, since the Tandoori Indian restaurant incident, and the last time I had rung his doorbell I had been there to defend poor Kaplovsky, who had been robbed of his housekeeper (and much more) who — the housekeeper, I mean — ended up, after a series of strange circumstances, being my housekeeper. But the situation was different now, and I felt confident of a renewal of friendship just as I felt a burning desire, a compulsion almost, to find out about Marie-Ève and Kaplovsky and my old friend Norris, to be involved again. Yet, strangely enough, when Norris opened the door, he said simply, "Ah, you've come. I didn't think you'd have gotten my message so soon." There had, of course, been no message. Norris then added, in a clipped, emotionless voice, "He's dead. He died in his sleep with his cats around him. We must go and tell Marie-Ève."

At first I had not the slightest idea who Norris might be talking about nor, for that matter, any memory of why I had come. And all I could think of was the first time Kaplovsky came to my apartment. He was immaculate, gracious and ghostly, and, after we had dispensed with the formality of the book of chess problems, he had taken from his pocket a photograph of a young woman who I took to be Angie Gosselin but who turned out to be Kaplovsky's young wife, Marie-Ève, in Mexico when they were first married. She was beautiful, intense and sad-looking and strangely familiar. It gave me a pang to see her. Kaplovsky luckily failed to notice my discomposure, or, and this is what I think now, he was completely aware of it and took it into account when he began to speak. He said, "I have always been in love with her, you know. Even before I met her — impossible love." "But surely," I said, "you can see her. She wishes it." "Ah," said Kaplovsky, "you've been talking to Norris."

Norris was dressed in a sombre suit with a watch on a fob-chain. His head was nearly bald, but his pencil-line moustache looked freshly trimmed, almost military in its precision, two upper case Ls on their backs with their feet together in the centre. His hands and face were covered with recent scratches, cat scratches it looked like, painted with orange disinfectant. "Who?" I asked, weakly. "Our poor friend Kaplovsky," said Norris. "He may have committed suicide. There was an empty bottle of barbiturates beside him. You know how it was with him." And I thought then that Norris had killed him, that Norris had stolen everything from Kaplovsky, everything including his ideas, his emotions, his wife and even his housekeeper.

Norris had published nothing since "Lunar Sensitivities," though that single paper had been sufficient to secure him a place in the textbooks and scientific histories, had indeed spawned a whole line of current research, had sent dozens of scholars searching for obscure rhythmic effects underlying natural phenomena. In the New Age bookstores, you could often find a section called simply "The Norris Effect" or "Lunar Studies." There had once been talk of a Public Television series in the United States. Norris himself scoffed at the popularization of his (Kaplovsky's) ideas, but on the rare occasions when we had spoken of his celebrity, he had reddened and affected a strange half-smile, not unlike the smile Kaplovsky himself wore when arguing chess theory or gene-splicing or New Music or even bivalve research those evenings long ago at the Tandoori Indian restaurant.

It is clear to me now that Kaplovsky did not think much of Norris's work, that his smile indicated an attitude of ironic condescension — how well I recall that Nicolas Cage gaffe. I myself had begun to despise Norris at that moment, though paradoxically I also pitied and admired him for his purely human will to prevail, to test himself, to put himself forward at any cost, warts and all. During the first of his two visits to my apartment, the untouched orange slices, sesame seed cakes and Chartreuse before him, his nervous hands making maps in the air, Kaplovsky said, "Norris isn't very graceful, you know. I keep thinking of how babies are born without the ability to see shapes or recognize objects. They don't know the difference between I and the world, themselves and their mothers. That's Norris all over."

We took a taxi from Norris's apartment to a convalescent home on the West Island, a place of high privet hedges, iron gates, discretion and money, a place out of time. The air was crisp and Victorian. Beyond the main building with its turrets and gables and gracious bow windows lay a vast acreage of gardens, greenhouses, shaded pathways, fountains and classical statuary. One expected to see nursing sisters in white gowns and caps wheeling invalids in cane-back chairs over the immaculate grounds. As we rolled up the semicircular drive, Norris said, "She has been here more than twenty years. She might have left at any time but prefers the seclusion and safety of St. Mildred's."

Through an open window, we could hear someone playing the violin. I gave Norris a look of inquiry, and he nodded. The scratches on his face and hands seemed to throb. Beads of sweat formed on his brow. I was reminded once again how alike we were, how in both of us a facade of correctness and discipline, of tweedy civility so characteristic of Montreal's old Anglo elite, concealed a passionate and wilful nature. "How did he die?" I asked, my voice descending to a husky whisper. "Tell me again." Norris didn't answer me. His eyes strayed to the upstairs window from which the celestial music emanated.

I say celestial, which it was, though oddly laboured or crippled in the fingering. And the music itself was strange, atonal and without apparent melody, something like the New Music concerts Kaplovsky had always spoken of with such enthusiasm. Everything in the performance seemed to be pressing against a barrier — of form, of physical infirmity, of emotional loss? I could not tell.

"She has never left these grounds?" I asked. He nodded his head gravely. "But, my dear Norris, that's a lie," I exclaimed. "I saw you and Marie-Ève at the Tandoori Indian restaurant a month ago smoking cigarettes. It has taken me that long to get over the shock. It's the Angie Gosselin episode all over again, only infinitely worse. You have betrayed us all."

Norris said nothing. His eyes remained fixed in the direction of that window. He tapped his fingers irritably against the crease of his trousers. Briefly, I doubted myself, my whole bizarre, if not to say paranoiac, fantasy of trysts, misalliance and now murder. But then I sensed a sea change within Norris, a relaxation of the inner being as it were, as though he were relieved that the truth was out. And I remembered again why I had liked him, what I had missed so much during the years we were apart — a certain childlike openness coupled with his predictable, and hence subversively charming, egoism. Norris was always naively and unaffectedly surprised to find himself in error or not quite the centre of attention he had assumed himself to be.

We waited for Marie-Ève in a front parlour crowded with horsehair chaise longues, graceful glassware, ivory chess sets, aspidistra, Christmas cactus and ancient cases full of stuffed song birds, exactly the decor I remembered from a hundred childhood visits to my grandmother's house in Westmount. It seemed, yes, as though we had entered the heart of something, and I felt an access of anticipation which was yet shot through with dread. Norris took a cigarette from a silver case on the coffee table and began to smoke — again that obscene gesture, the cigarette between his third and fourth fingers, his face half-hidden, all this rendered somewhat comic or even mawkish by the cat scratches and the disinfectant stains.

He said, "You will ask yourself, Who pays for all this? Not Kaplovsky, surely, on his pathetic assistantships. When I found her, she was living in a halfway house where they assigned patients deemed no longer a threat to themselves or others. The place was filthy, graffiti covered the walls. She was over-medicated and owned just one set of clothes. Everyone had abandoned her, even the doctors. I brought her here. At first, I did what I did for Kaplovsky. I thought I could bring them together, but soon I fell in love with her myself. I grew to despise my friend because he would not take advantage of his good fortune and take her back and because he would not make her happy. And then I grew to hate her for her constancy, which was a kind of madness."

I listened to Norris with a growing sense of horror and pity. The Angie Gosselin affair had been but the proverbial tip of the iceberg, my own malign part as unwitting and determined as a cog in some complex machine of desire. Once again, a mysterious phrase came unbidden to my thoughts — "Original Sin." But before I could examine the words in the context of my relations with Norris and

Kaplovsky, the parlour door opened, and Norris motioned me to silence.

The beautiful young woman I had observed at the Tandoori Indian restaurant a month before entered the room, her misshapen left arm still encased in that elegant black glove. Perhaps she had taken it off to play, for she was still in the process of pulling it up past her elbow when she came through the door. The thought of that naked, mangled hand unaccountably filled me with brutal and sudden lust.

Norris's face was a mask of livid scratches and orange paint. He seemed suddenly pathetic, lost. He spoke to her directly in tones both familiar and intimate, as though they were brother and sister, tones which inspired in me paroxysms of jealousy. She listened in silence to the story of the death of her lover, Norris's story, which I took to be a tissue of lies. I imagined something entirely different from the lonely, quiet death Norris described. I imagined Norris calmly mixing the fatal cocktail, administering the posset of cognac and barbiturates to the passive and unwitting Kaplovsky by the dim light of the bedside lamp, books, old clothes, ancient newspapers strewn about the room, the cats cowering in dark corners.

I imagined Norris's impatience as the drugs failed to take immediate effect, imagined him struggling over Kaplovsky with a pillow, Kaplovsky's legs and arms jerking, the cats now aroused, mad with terror, spitting and hissing and throwing themselves at the murderer, their mad shadows on the wall, the dull thuds of their bodies, Norris's gasps, the final quiet which settled like a blanket and seemed endless.

Did he suspect that he had just destroyed the best part of himself? Or had he come to regard Kaplovsky as a demonic presence, source of all temptation and evil? Were Kaplovsky's struggles real attempts to save himself, or were they merely the reflexes of a dying animal? Was this, finally, an act of love between the two men? Or was it just the climax in a series of violent interactions, a duel to the death?

As Norris's voice droned on, I lapsed into an utterly Kaplovskian reverie upon the roots of desire and violence and the pathos of the poor self which loses its identity the moment it reaches for the thing it needs to live. And I was reminded of the constant, vituperative sovereignty debates for which our country is famous, the ebb and flow of marching feet that formed a backdrop to Kaplovsky's personal tragedy and to which he was always looking for clues and analogies. In my mind, we were coming closer and closer to the state of that increasingly rare Long Point Bay mussel (now ever more possibly extinct) in its endless, rhythmic dance of love. Once, peering intently out the snow-battered window of the Tandoori Indian restaurant into the darkness beyond, Kaplovsky exclaimed, "What is it?" His voice betrayed an astonished eagerness, and, as Norris later agreed, we all three suddenly had the same intense sensation that we were hanging by some fragile thread over a mysterious dark torrent.

Marie-Ève had risen from the chair in which she sat to receive the news. She stood with her back to us, her wounded arm cradled in front of her, a cigarette smouldering forgotten in her dead fingers. At length, she turned to us and reached with her good hand to pluck something from her lips, a crumb of tobacco from her cigarette perhaps. She began to speak but in Canadian French, the quick, elided national argot, which, though I had lived all my life in this city, I had never learned. She addressed Norris in tones that were at once dismissive and vexed, tones that reminded me more of a slatternly cleaning lady than an educated woman of elegance and distinction.

Norris hung his head, responding to a series of questions with successive nods which left him bent over, staring at the floor. I understood a word here and there as she jabbed the air with that gloved hand and cigarette. Chief among them was the noun "meurtrier," from which I deduced that she shared my suspicions about Kaplovsky's death. But her attitude struck me as wrong, as did Norris's — she might as well have been arguing with a cab driver or the man who did her dry cleaning. And Norris seemed cowed, more like a small boy having his knuckles rapped for looking at dirty pictures than a man who had just disclosed the death of a lifelong lover.

Where was the mystery, romance and passion of which I had heard so much in the long years preceding this moment? I felt the hair rise on the back of my neck as I began to understand how mundane and small poor Kaplovsky's death appeared to those who had loved him the most, nothing more, really, than getting the starch order wrong on a beloved dress. At the same time, I was insanely jealous of Norris and the monstrous masochistic intimacy he had achieved with Marie-Ève. Her words were like whips and caresses and carried no hint of warmth either toward Norris or Kaplovsky (how she reminded me of Angie Gosselin, who could have been her double, aside from a few years difference in age and that broken hand).

Norris's rubicund face seemed about to explode in orgasmic bliss, though his eyes remained fixed upon the hardwood floor. In that horrid moment, I nearly ran, nearly left them there in their attitude of fetid triumph. But then I thought, He won't live long. Then who will pay to keep her? And I knew, suddenly, that I had won, that I had achieved the magical nexus of violence, vengeance and power that is the root of modern love.

I rose from my seat, my eyes shining with desire, and took a step towards Marie-Ève (her gloved arm like a diagonal splash of ink across her torso, rendering her null, like a cancelled stamp). But she ignored me. Save for one cold glance, she continued berating poor Norris. Her face was full of light, full of a perverse excitement, not, I thought, because she loved Kaplovsky or Norris or anyone else for that matter, but because the idea of Kaplovsky and her loyalty to that idea gave her life colour, drama and meaning just as Kaplovsky had given Norris everything that was essentially interesting in his existence. And for one withering moment I understood what Kaplovsky meant when he spoke so passionately of liberating himself from love.

2

A DAY LATER, I met Norris at the doorway of Harvey's on St. Catherine Street, then walked with him in silence to the church which, as he told me, was not far off. I marvelled at the intuition, the dream, as it were, that had led me to Norris's door, and marvelled still more when we came to the Catholic church from which Kaplovsky was to be buried. "Yes," Norris said, seeing my face, "he had everything — love, his work and God."

He sounded bitter. His cat scratches seemed livid with infection. Organ music swelled within. An odd assortment of mourners crowded the pews, including well-known biologists from the university along with a small phalanx of Kaplovsky's fellow programmers, Asians mostly, and, surprisingly, several men and women, who I recognized as having worked at the Tandoori Indian restaurant when it was our regular haunt.

Kaplovsky was there in a simple box. I was anxious to see him one last time, his arms folded in some ungenuine pose, his pale face reserved but betraying his perpetual attitude to life with that enigmatic half-smile. But in death his face had taken on a ravaged, pinched expression. Mortuary makeup did little to conceal a lurid hematoma under his left eye, a swollen and cracked lower lip. His right ear had been stitched inexpertly and the stitches hidden beneath his hair. A stained silk scarf wrapped around his neck seemed meant to conceal some further injury (yes, in spite of what Norris had said, anyone could see Kaplovsky's death had not been peaceful).

Two women waited for us in an otherwise empty pew near the front. I recognized Marie-Ève immediately, but Angie Gosselin took me a moment or two. I had not seen her since she abandoned me. To be truthful I had never recovered from Angie; she had shaken me to my roots. When she left me (because, as she said at the time, she could not find me, find my heart), I turned inward, becoming reclusive, misanthropic and depressive. Nothing broke the spell — not psychotherapy or drugs or occasional hospital-ization — until that day when I passed the Tandoori Indian restaurant and happened to spy Norris and Marie-Ève seated at our habitual table. And I remembered just then something Kaplovsky said to Norris after a particularly wounding debate over New Music during which Norris had begun to sweat profusely, fidget with his collar, jab the table with his fingertip and rub his eyes with the heels of his palms until he finally spilled a bottle of Indian beer onto his lap. Kaplovsky had said, "We must learn to love the dreamer, not the dream."

What he meant by this I have no idea, but I wanted to speak of it to Norris, could barely restrain myself because of the circumstances. I was overcome by the strange Orphean dissonances of the organ, notes that seemed to clash and scatter like sparks in a steel mill, then zigzag upwards like a hundred butterflies, light as air, light as light. Angie leaned into me and grasped my hand. "He wrote that, you know," she said, an assertion which caused me no end of irritation. And, of course, I remembered that I had heard this same music just the day before as we waited outside St. Mildred's and the sound of Marie-Ève's violin drifted down to us from the window.

Norris seemed overcome as well, his throat contracting in an effort to still his emotions. I thought how empty I had felt when I finally won Angie from my friend's grasp. How much worse Norris had felt, I cannot say. That Kaplovsky had understood this seemed also indubitable, just as I am sure he would have understood the present moment and his own role in our common tragedy. I looked at my friend Norris, who suddenly seemed transparent or dia-phanous. (Looking into the mirror that morning, I had thought, People can see right through me. What did it mean?) I could almost see the blood pumping beneath Norris's skin. He seemed almost to be fading away, and I could hear him thinking, thinking enviously that Kaplovsky had once more achieved precedence — it was his funeral after all. Kaplovsky was the true original, the one with panache, always leading the way into the unknown. Never mind that Norris had murdered him with a pillow or possibly a piece of electrical cord, had summarily and violently thrust him into the unknown.

It occurred to me that perhaps it had always been this way, that Kaplovsky had always fed in some obscure way off Norris's jealousy, that he had become himself, as it were, in order to humiliate his friend, that we were all created by this strange conjunction of friendship, desire and envy. And here we were, assembled for the necessary last act, the alter egos, who would never again be together as we were now.

As we stumbled outside into the rain-lashed streets of Montreal, I felt Angie clasp my hand again. (Kaplovsky said all the great Canadian writers come from Montreal and they are all dark Romantics, that Montreal is the City of Love, that it proves how love is the arena of self-making for the West — as I remembered this, there were Separatists and Federalists marching against each other along St. Catherine Street, marching to meet in the old cholera boneyard at Dominion Square.) She nodded toward Norris, who looked suddenly moribund, and again I was certain he would not live much longer. Marie-Ève seemed fragile, brittle, wounded, despairing — utterly ravishing, I thought. The church doors up the stone steps behind us, gaping like the gates to the Land of the Dead, seemed reluctant to let us leave.

Norris suggested a meal at a restaurant nearby, but, before we had gone more than a few steps in that direction, he began to complain of nausea, a peculiar weakness in his limbs, headache. His eyes were feverish. His cat scratches seemed, if anything, more inflamed.

We took a cab to his apartment, which, he warned us apologetically, had been in disarray since Kaplovsky's death. The odours of cat urine and tinned cat food assailed our nostrils at the entry. Cats ran hissing and spitting at the sight of Norris, slinking along the baseboards, concealing themselves beneath the threadbare Bauhaus chairs, the table where Norris worked (papers and books piled high but yellow with age and dust), the bed in the adjoining room, and inside his closets and open cupboards. Crusty, half-eaten tins of cat food and brimming litter boxes dotted the floors. Kaplovsky's cats had been left homeless and starving, he explained. There was no alternative except for Norris to bring them home temporarily. They had even tried to kill his own one-eyed tabby. He gestured helplessly with his wounded hands. He was afraid to sleep at night lest they should attack him in his dreams.

I saw Angie's hand go to her mouth. Marie-Ève seemed stunned. I felt the dizziness one always feels in the face of madness, the sense of being on a precipice, at the edge of an abyss. Norris stumbled into the bedroom and dropped onto the untidy sheets with an arm over his eyes, his lungs heaving desperately for air. Three cats bolted from beneath the bed with a single screech. Plainly they hated and feared my friend. The spirit of Kaplovsky was everywhere in the apartment, from the malignant odours to the overwhelming terror of the cats, their skulking, cowering ways, their eyes that reminded me of Kaplovsky's as he crept away from my door, oh so long ago.

Norris looked like a corpse, emaciated and waxy, with the orange tracery of his cat scratches disappearing beneath his clothing. Marie-Ève knelt beside the bed and placed her gloved hand on the pillow behind his head. It was more tenderness than I had come to expect of her, yet Norris failed to notice. I could no longer guess her motivation, although it seemed to me we had all approached the mystery, detected some hint of the shape or pattern which connected us to one another and guided our every gesture. Perhaps watching Norris, Marie-Ève had lost her former certainty, her sense of self-possession (albeit thinly based on a paradox — her non-relationship with the evasive and agoraphobic Kaplovsky). Perhaps she now saw Norris's decline as a precursor of her own inelegant and ineluctable fate.

A clatter of dishware from the kitchen drew me from the scene in the bedroom. I found Angie, rubber-gloved, with a cigarette in her mouth (she smoked an alien brand — American Spirit), rinsing cat food tins in the sink in preparation for recycling, collecting the over-flowing contents of litter boxes in garbage bags, dusting, wiping and organizing. She had the cats eating fresh food off saucers at her feet, rubbing themselves against her legs. And I remembered the warmth of her hand at the church, the insistence of her intimacy, as though all those years of separation had passed in a moment. She said, "I'm married now — to a sculptor, half-Montagnais, from the Côte du Nord. He builds everything out of ice so it melts in the summer. Out of nothing, back to nothing. Very Indian. We have three little boys." She slipped off her gloves, tapped her cigarette ash into an empty cat food tin, and plucked a fragment of tobacco from her lip, a gesture which reminded me so much of Marie-Ève that I was momentarily unbalanced. I was in love with both women, although, in a peculiar way, they seemed to be the same woman, the same object of desire (I would be the first to admit that in certain superficial ways — wounded hand, marriage, children, career choice, age, place of birth among others — they differed markedly).

Norris, my friend, my mentor, my confidant, for years the closest thing I had to a father or brother, lay wasting away in the next room. I was as confused as anyone at the sudden and dreamlike turn of events, yet, when I looked back on my life, I could not remember a time when events had been other than sudden and dreamlike. And I recalled with a dismal sense of irony the conviction with which I had set out to visit Norris the day before.

The sound of muffled sobs came from the bedroom; Norris or Marie-Ève, I could not tell. Police sirens hummed uneasily in distant streets. The sounds of marching feet, ragged cheers, voices raised in passion and amplified over bullhorns drifted further and further away. I felt my old fear of open spaces beginning to return and found myself backing toward the wall with its strange clam-shell-patterned wallpaper.

I remembered then how, when Angie and I were together, we would walk on Mount Royal Sunday mornings, holding hands or arm-in-arm, eat croissants and drink coffee in an Italian coffee shop just off Avenue du Parc, read the papers, go to the cinema in the afternoon or take in a New Music concert, make love through the dinner hour and then adjourn to La Carreta on St. Zotique for a meal of *pupusas* and beer. Once or twice, we thought we were followed, shadowed, as they say in detective movies. The world had seemed ineffably beautiful then, just as it did now in Norris's kitchen — beautiful, sad and mysterious, with a Twilight of the Gods quality one could not explain other than to say that we cannot exist without seeing ourselves as gods or great heroes of myth or as the First Men to walk the earth. It was a thought worthy of Kaplovsky himself. And I had a burning, pointless desire to tell Norris, as though having the thought were not enough, as though the thought itself would not exist unless I told Norris (or his friend). But then I felt an equally strong yet contrary impulse to keep quiet, perhaps even to run away, save myself, escape.

Yet there was no escape. In the gathering gloom (night was falling), I could hear the howls of distant wolves. Across the continent, ancient dogs were taking up the lament, lifting their faces to the moon. Deep in a thousand ageless lakes, tiny invertebrates shivered and rocked in their nacreous cradles, anxious to resume their purposeless journey. Angie Gosselin looked, in the dim light of the darkening kitchen, like the Queen of Night herself. An enigmatic smile played across her lips, secretive and mysterious.

I suddenly wanted to know the names of her children. Her husband. I wanted to know what the years away from me had been like. Did she still draw and paint? Did she still have the little Tarot deck I gave her and her collection of books on witchcraft? At bedtime, did she still run twice to the bathroom to pee — just to be sure? I opened my mouth to ask, but words suddenly failed me. Beyond the sounds of Norris's groans and Marie-Ève's weeping, there was only silence and an infinite lunar stillness, inside and out.

State of the Nation

WE IN THE REPUBLIC are exhausted.

Our enemies have lain down their arms, leaving us suddenly without a national purpose.

Brown people are pouring over the border to take up work we heedlessly relinquish in our pursuit of leisure and sexual gratification.

Nights I drive down the coast road to the marshes at the mouth of the Tijuana River and park and watch them crawling across the border like insects.

The country is awash in brown people and perverts of all kinds.

The fat woman across the street (we are four storeys up) has pushed her bed to the window and lolls there naked, exposing herself, masturbating shamelessly with an assortment of household objects: salamis, broom handles, cat brushes, vacuum cleaner attachments, bits of broken furniture, aerosol cans, stereo albums, pizza cutters and cork screws.

Sometimes she simply lies with her head thrown back in ecstasy, holding the lips of her vulva open.

This is an electrifying development, let me tell you.

All of a sudden, I have an attention span again.

Prior to this, I often couldn't think of a reason to go out or stay in (except at night when the sewagy, rotting smell of the Tijuana wafted me southwards along the coast road). Occasionally, I have stood before the door for hours on end, trying to decide what to do.

Now I race to get up before she does, shower and comb my hair, then dash down the stairs for a box of week-old raspberry Danish pastries, five pounds of salted peanuts and a dozen Mexican beers. Usually I am in position, stretched on my Naugahyde recliner in front of the window, before she stirs, before she thrusts the first dainty foot from beneath her soiled pink sheets.

Sometimes she waves.

On one hand, I keep a cooler for the beer, a carton of Marlboros, a slab of Irish butter, my pastries and peanuts. On the other, I have a large steel garbage can (I am a firm believer in design efficiency).

I throw the trash — bottles, rinds, husks, butts, packaging, spent matches — into the garbage can, which occasionally leads to minor fires that annoy the neighbours but cause no more harm than a little localized air pollution and a mark like a storm cloud on my ceiling.

Once I woke up to find the hair on the left side of my head blazing like a fatwood torch.

One day we meet accidentally in the greeting card shop at the corner (I go there to read — I can't get through a whole book anymore).

I'm abashed. I have nothing to say.

She says, Are you the guy with the telescope?

I nod. I am wearing a leather World War I aviator's helmet with goggles, a white silk scarf, yellow shorts printed with nodding palm fronds and Birkenstocks.

I don't want to fuck you, she says. I want things to go on just as they are. You understand? Only I want to see you too. Everything. I have binoculars. I'll watch.

A purulent musk assails my nostrils. Sweat pools in deltas under her arms, slides down the side of her nose like translucent snails.

Her eyes roll up in terror.

She flails the air with her arms, then tilts backward into an array of comic wedding anniversary cards and crashes to the floor.

I can see what effort this terse communication has cost her. This access of vulnerability has its own peculiar allure.

And I rush away in a panic, fearing nothing so much as love and the loss of love, worried above all else that, having revealed herself, she will now retreat into the spell of anonymity by which we all protect ourselves from hurt.

But things go on just as before.

Except that now I strip off and parade myself in front of the window from time to time and wave.

She no longer waves back. Engrossed as she is in her pleasure, she rarely has a hand to spare.

Then she tries to kill herself. She lets me watch the whole thing, ripping up sheets to tie off her arms, slicing her wrists vertically instead of horizontally in order to avoid severing the tendons, then letting the blood spurt in a decreasing trajectory over her thighs and sheets.

After a while, I call 911 and save her life.

One of the EMS guys vomits when he enters her apartment. From what I can see, she is not much of a neatness freak.

In the hospital, she mistakes me for someone else, someone named Buddy.

From internal evidence, I conclude that Buddy is her brother, that he disappeared twenty-two years ago after accidentally shooting a boy named Natrone Hales to death in the family garage. The boys were twelve at the time.

I have brought her a spring posy from a gift shop downstairs operated by a blind person who reads the money with his fingers. I got eighty-two dollars in change from a ten-dollar bill.

Presently, she begins to yell at me for going off like that, for never sending a postcard.

I say I called twice, both times on her birthday, and both times I hung up when she answered.

She looks at me. Her features soften. She says I called more than twice like that.

I say, yeah.

You look about the same, she says.

I tell her about the man who held me in a closet for eight years against my will, the time in the hospital, the girl I loved who died of anthrax, the accident with the car when I had no insurance and had to pay off the kid's medical bills holding down three jobs and how he used to come around in that custom wheelchair and taunt me, about my time in Nam, my self-esteem problems, the hole in my nose from drugs, my bladder spasms.

What happened to your hair?

A fire, I say.

I say, I don't think you really know me.

Oh, Buddy, Buddy, Buddy, she says.

I try to lie down beside her on the bed, but there is no beside her. I end up on the floor.

Why did you do that? she asks. You haven't changed.

Who will you want me to be tomorrow? I think, as I leave, realizing that there is a mystery here, a truth about the nature of love, that we are always falling in love with some picture, that the real person eludes us, though he is always jumping up and down in the background, waving his arms and shouting for attention — someone has turned off the sound.

Mostly, I am afraid that with my luck the real Buddy will walk through the door at any minute now.

In *Time* magazine, I read that the Buddhists call this place the hungry-ghost world.

On the way out of the hospital, I ask the blind guy at the gift shop for change for a twenty. I give him a five and get forty-nine dollars back.

You made a mistake, I say.

He gives me another ten.

I don't get down to the hospital for a week because I can't figure out who I think she is, maybe just one of those multiple-personality sluts you meet in the bars these days, women who give you five percent of their souls and take no responsibility.

When I do go, she is sitting up in bed with a food tray. She has combed her hair, she's wearing a pink nightgown, she's lost weight.

Ominously, they have untied her hands.

She smiles and says, I'm glad you stopped by.

The voice of total insanity, I think.

I got something for you, she says, handing me a gift-wrapped parcel.

It's a new universal remote for my TV and entertainment centre.

I nearly weep with gratitude. No one has ever given me a present before.

Then I recall that I'm not sure who I am supposed to be today.

She says, A year ago I was a nurse in Arizona. One day, an old prospector drove down out of the Two Heads mountains to drop off a ten-year-old Apache girl he'd bought and got pregnant.

He said we could do what we wanted with her. He just couldn't use her now that she was pregnant. He'd have to go and get another.

The Apache girl didn't even know she was pregnant. The doctors delivered her, then put both of them up for adoption — without ever telling the girl what had really happened to her.

I kept thinking about her, that this important thing had occurred without her knowing it, that somewhere there was another person closer to her than life, without either of them being aware of it. I imagined she must have been haunted by a feeling of something just out of reach, a mystery without a name.

I asked myself, What if, later on, she were to meet her child in the street? Would she just pass by? Or would she feel tugged toward him?

She stops talking for a moment, looks a little frightened.

I say, That's exactly the relationship I have with reality most days.

She smiles again and says, I guess I cracked up. I believe drugs and alcohol were involved. They are most of the time.

You mean you're normal now? I ask.

You're not Buddy, are you?

I am out of there, a crushing weight on my chest — heartburn or love, I can't tell which.

The blind guy at the gift shop is watching the local news on TV with the volume on high torque. A band of Yuma Indians on the border near Nogales has just sold its tribal land to the city of San Diego for a landfill and plans to use the money to start a casino.

We should put 'em on a boat and send 'em back where they came from, he says.

I ask for a Snickers bar and give him a five.

He gives me back four Jacksons and change.

I say, I can't take this. You counted wrong.

Oh boy, he says. Just checking. I got burned twice last week. Called the cops. Eight of them got the place staked out right now, waiting for my signal.

Don't die, I think, suddenly fearful.

I click back to CNN and catch the news from the Republic of Paranoia, where only victims are citizens with rights.

Hell, our army won't even consider fighting a country where the people can afford shoes anymore.

I knew a woman once who said love is nothing but a mechanism for heat exchange.

She said, We are just roadkill on the highway to nowhere.

I click the remote and see myself as a slim young man with a future. I see my country, violent and innocent again, like a flash of sheet lightning in history. I see her cradling a child to her breast, the child feeling absolutely safe and unafraid.

I think, Sadness, sadness, sadness.

A Piece of the True Cross

I

MY SISTER, DARLA, was struck by lightning the summer we bought the house on Block Island.

She wasn't killed, and now, twenty years later, she is married to an investment banker named Tad and has two healthy sons. She complains of deafness in her left ear and a residual ache in her left elbow and shoulder. She is apprehensive when storms approach. She claims sometimes to see auras around peoples' heads. A lot of people claim to see auras, but I generally disbelieve them. Darla I believe.

I was thirteen that year, and the world seemed an ineffably sad and lonely place to me. Our father had founded a chemical company with plants in Georgia and Louisiana. He had come from the South, those were his roots, but he had never taken us back for so much as a visit. Summers we usually went to Nantucket or Provincetown, until we bought the old Waring place on Block Island. I spent my falls, winters and springs at a boarding school in the Berkshires.

I was standing at my bedroom window watching storm clouds advance over the sound when the lightning struck our house. More distant bolts were etching maps in the sky. I had just spotted one that looked so much like the Mississippi River I could pinpoint where the family fertilizer factory stood, down by the delta.

I imagined the delta heat and humidity; I imagined elderly

black men with floppy-eared dogs sitting before ramshackle clapboard houses, spitting and nodding to me as I rode by on my bicycle; I imagined fishing for catfish in the bayous on long mosquito-filled evenings. But I failed to notice at once that the Mississippi of my imagination had struck dangerously close to the house. It hung there a moment, illuminating everything in a brilliant chiaroscuro, until the clap of thunder broke over my head.

Almost at once a second clap erupted through the ceiling of my room. A ball of fire the size of a tennis ball hovered over the metal bedstead, then split in two and traveled along the frame and across the painted plank floor before climbing the pipes of my bedroom sink. With amazement and delight, I watched it recombine and spiral into the sink, disappearing down the drain hole. With a loud pop, the sink exploded away from the wall, dangling free on its pipes, a cloud of plaster dust mushrooming up from the floor.

From elsewhere in the house, there came the sounds of splintering glass and wood. On the floor below, Mother began to scream, filling me with irritation and dread.

I was so confused I could only turn again to the window to watch the play of light and dark on last year's dead leaves swirling above the broken stone walk, the skewed croquet pins in the lawn and the dying elm tree next to the mysterious octagonal carriage house with the revolving floor and the garret apartment where St. John Waring's mistress had once lived in luxury and car fumes.

Just below, the gardener's elderly black Lab, Sukey, raced her sinister shadow past the juniper bushes, her tongue lolling in fright.

Then, hearing Father's grumpy, short-winded imprecations and his heavy feet on the stairs, I finally ran to the hall doorway and peered out. The house was dark, the electricity having failed when the storm began. Lightning struck again, bursting white from the hall-end window. The pungent odours of smoke and singed hair penetrated my nostrils.

I saw Mother standing at Darla's door, her face a pale mask of horror, her mouth open, everything white and black.

. . .

The old Waring place was to be our summer home from then on.

The Warings, who had once been very rich, built the house with the intention of establishing a permanent family seat on the model of the old English country home, a refuge and retreat for succeeding generations of Warings stretching into the millennium. But Grace Waring, the widow, had closed the house after St. John's death, mostly because of that mistress and her bitter memories.

When she died, a son sold the estate for taxes, and for a time it had served as a tuberculosis sanatorium, hence the metal bedsteads and the chipped enamel sinks in every room.

The basement and attic concealed more macabre vestiges of those sad years: kidney-shaped bed pans and spit dishes, musty cardboard crates of patient records, bales of blank admission forms, a pyramid of unexposed x-ray film, the frame of the old x-ray machine, and neatly stapled files of invoices (for fresh vegetables from the local farmers, a keg of nails and a dozen copper pipe elbows from the hardware store in the village, gas and per diems for a doctor's trip to a medical convention in New Haven — homely things oddly unconnected with death).

These parts of the house were considered closed off by my parents, who seemed to have gotten an idea from their real estate agent that doors had been nailed up or bricked over, that whole wings had been condemned (this is why, they congratulated themselves, they had been able to buy it so cheaply), though, in fact, Darla and I wandered in there for days on end, alternately chilled and fascinated by each grisly discovery.

The last owners before we moved in the summer the lightning struck Darla were a French-Canadian family called La Douceur, a madcap bunch, by all accounts, who, when they abandoned the place, left behind a large assortment of beach furniture, a roomful of fake Japanese screens bought at a sale when the 1967 World's Fair closed in Montreal, a fieldstone and concrete shrine on the front lawn with a statue of the Virgin Mary in a niche, and their grand-mother's ashes.

We only learned about the ashes a week after our arrival, when Mr. La Douceur telephoned from Quebec City in a panic.

Mother sent me racing upstairs to a room marked LINEN, where, in a back corner of a wall cabinet, I found a copper urn about the size and shape of a bowling pin. The urn smelled vaguely medicinal, as did almost everything in that house. The ashes made the sound of sand shifting.

When I looked up there was a stranger, a gaunt young woman wrapped in a sheet, like a mummy, I thought, standing in the doorway watching me. She had black eyebrows like bits of charcoal and wide, feverish eyes that gazed at me with startled affection. When she saw that I saw her, she smiled slightly, wearily, it seemed, then turned and vanished down the hall. Clumsy with the weight of the La Douceur family ashes, I ran to the door, but the woman was nowhere to be seen.

Reluctantly, I returned to the wall cabinet, where, just as she appeared, I had noticed something hidden on the shelf behind the urn. I reached up and fished out a clear plastic plaque with a jagged splinter of wood embedded in it. On the plaque backing, behind the splinter, there was an illustration of the Sacred Heart. Turning the plaque over, I found a legend printed in Gothic script: A Piece of the True Cross.

Later, when I told Darla about the woman in the white sheet and showed her the relic, she seemed unsurprised.

Darla was two years older than me, and it was about this time that she tried to have sexual intercourse with me in one of the eight bathrooms distributed amongst the upstairs bedrooms. This was our one and only attempt at physical intimacy, and it was unsuccess-ful (to be precise, I did not attain complete erection, and my bladder sphincter relaxed out of nervousness just as I entered her vagina, causing us both a good deal of embarrassment).

Mr. La Douceur arrived a week later, alone in the family station wagon, to retrieve his mother's ashes, sweaty, self-important and evincing little embarrassment at forgetting such an important item. Though there were several Japanese screens in evidence (Mother having decided she liked them as an interior decoration for breaking up the vast spaces and sight lines of the living room), he did not mention them. And he drove away quickly without a nod to the Virgin Mary.

Once a year Father had the basal cell cancers removed from his nose and forehead, his face becoming a pattern of red skin and flesh-coloured bandages. ("Quite a sight," Darla would say.) The last time I saw him was at the opening of a show of my paintings at Verna Walter's gallery in Soho, when he came through the door with his face bandaged, wearing a dinner jacket and carpet slippers.

Offering him a glass of champagne, I whispered huffily, "You always have to make yourself the centre of attention."

He blinked but did not reply, though I believe he understood what I meant, the whole depth and breadth of my lifelong accusation.

He was nearly blind by then and chronically depressed. He wore thick spectacles and read with difficulty, with the aid of a magnifying glass. This blindness contributed to his death three years ago, when he spilled something in a lab and the whole Louisiana factory went up. What was left of him could have fit easily in Madame La Douceur's urn.

I have his glasses, though.

Mother was mesmerizing, energetic, directionless and hysterical. When I was sad, Mother tore her clothes. When I was angry, Mother punished me. She was forever exhorting me to *do* things with the accent and enthusiasm of a girls' school field hockey coach (a tone Darla gradually acquired when it came to raising her own sons).

I would never have skied, played softball or ice hockey, sung in the St. John the Apostle choir (where I was fondled, pleasantly enough, by a lay brother named Peter McNab), gone out on dates or learned to paint if it hadn't been for Mother. I wouldn't have lived without her, Darla says, meaning "lived" figuratively.

Yet when my father died, she became a spent force.

Now, like me, she lives in the city. Once a week she telephones to ask what she should do, redecorate the living room or buy new china, go to Jamaica or take a tour of English pubs?

"Sell the old Waring place," I say.

But, like me, she never does anything.

Both my parents refused to see ghosts or anything else unusual about the summer house, or themselves for that matter (I was twenty-five before I realized there was nothing normal about my upbringing). They thought it was a sign when Darla did not die of lightning bolts. A miracle, Mother said, with her usual melo-dramatic flare.

I remember the three of us converging on Darla's door, the odours of singed hair, dry rot and ancient dust (since house dust is mainly sloughed off skin cells, Darla and I assumed we had been breathing dead TB patients the whole summer), and the sounds of glass breaking, clapboards tearing themselves from old square nails in agony and Mother's muffled shrieks.

Darla lay amidst her smouldering bedclothes, the hair on one side of her head burned down to the scalp, her window frame smashed in and dangling from the wall, shards of glass glittering on the floor and blankets every time the lightning flashed. Her left breast was bare, the nightdress torn or burned from her, and her nipple stood black and salient against the whiteness of her skin.

She looked like a queen of the dead, with her startled eyes, the black and white strobing of the lightning, the terrible music of the breaking glass.

Unable to see, Father stumbled forward with his arms outstretched (his magnified eyes peering everywhere, trying to identify who was a friend and what was dangerous).

Mother flung herself at his neck, crying inanely, "Oh, darling, I'll save you. I'll save you. Don't go near her."

Pushing past them, cutting my bare feet on the glass but feeling nothing, hypnotized by the beauty of the scene and the sense of strangeness, I touched Darla's forearm where it lay across her belly, half-expecting it to be cold in death, half-expecting it to jump with high voltage and drop me in my tracks. It was only then, in a flash of lightning, that I saw she was still breathing and that in her hand she clutched the La Douceur relic, the plasticized piece of the True Cross.

2

I AM THIRTY-THREE NOW. My private life is a disaster.

A year ago I gave Mother's Irish claddagh ring, the one my father gave her on their engagement (signifying love, friendship and loyalty), to a twenty-year-old leather boy who let me masturbate him in a peep show on 42nd Street. I did not know his name but believed, apparently without foundation, that we were in love.

For four years, I shared my loft and bed with an aspiring poet from Cleveland named Vicky Wonderlight, and though we kissed and cuddled and masturbated each other, we never made love (to be fair, this must reveal as much about Vicky's capacity for intimacy as mine).

I design and build museum exhibits for a living (growing up in my family, I had become accustomed to making old dead things the centre of my life), travelling around the country, sometimes sojourning for weeks in comfortingly anonymous motel rooms while I do my work.

Nights, I linger in my loft (now all my own) painting huge canvases that look, at first, almost preternaturally black. Yet, when held under a bright light, they come up in a dozen hues of electric blue-white and red.

The subjects are all the same, a naked man (self-portrait) falling in space. Around him swirl a number of objects, ash urns, thick wire-rimmed spectacles, croquet pins, old Daimler automobiles (of the kind that St. John Waring used to park beneath his mistress's apartment), iron bedsteads and enamelled bedroom sinks, choirboy vestments and lightning bolts and tennis ball-sized globes of light that dance upon his fingertips.

Always half-hidden somewhere in the chaotic background there is an object that resembles a plaque of clear plastic containing a splinter of wood (like a lightning bolt) to signify the miraculous quality of life, our slim hope of redemption.

These naked male figures are like ghosts. You can see through them, and their faces wear hurt expressions of puzzlement and nostalgia.

Darla always claimed to remember nothing of her near brush with death by electrocution. A doctor examined her, gave her a sedative by injection, and closed her eyes with his fingers. She slept for three days, and when she awoke she was deaf.

The deafness lasted a month and then gradually abated — though for years Darla was haunted by mysterious pops, grindings, clangs and echoes. My mother and father never noticed, except insofar as they grew irritated with her inattentiveness. I managed to cover for her most of the time, answering their questions, giving her furtive hand signals and exaggerating my lip movements when I could get away with it. Alone, we seemed to communicate tele-pathically. By touching hands and pointing, or looking into each other's eyes, we knew at once each other's most complicated thoughts.

Mother cut Darla's hair so that the singed areas did not seem so obvious, though for several weeks, Darla drew stares when she ventured into town on grocery-buying trips.

Because of her deafness and the hair and a certain timidity caused by her fear of storms (at first she had only to look up at a clear sky to be overcome with terror), she grew to depend on me completely.

One day I found her in the bathroom next to my room, naked, stinking and moaning, covered with her own feces which she had retrieved from the toilet and rubbed on herself. I cleaned her up and helped her to bed, where she slept the afternoon away, only to appear for dinner, clean and fresh-smelling, silent and inattentive.

That summer I lost my virginity to the gardener's son, Billy Dedankalus, a pale, thin young man who was terrified of the ghosts (though he had never seen one). I think now that I was in love without really knowing it. Sometimes I think that this was the one great love of my life, the pattern for all the rest. For Billy quickly fell in love with Darla and left me with my memories.

In the days following Darla's accident, while she was still confined to her room, I began wandering in the gardens, sometimes following the aging Sukey on her rounds, or in the abandoned hothouses where old Dendankalus, the gardener, kept a few beds for starting vegetables and a collection of rare cacti, huge in red earthenware pots on the rough wood tables.

At first silently and at a distance, I watched him work, admiring the ritualistic precision with which he dug, planted, weeded and pruned. Soon I began to help, working alongside him with my sleeves rolled up and sweat rolling down my flushed cheeks.

He was a lean, sinewy man, with a sun-browned, cadaverous face and thin, white hair cropped close like a convict's. He carried a rifle wherever he worked to shoot stray cats, ground hogs and rabbits that threatened his plantings. His intensity and off-hand cruelty both repelled and fascinated me.

He had first worked there as a boy, assisting a Japanese gardener the Warings imported from the city to lay out their estate. He had helped put in a pool where fat-cheeked goldfish swam and where the La Douceurs' Virgin Mary now stood contemplating her feet. Behind the house, where the shore dunes met the lawn, there were dwarf cedars Dedankalus had learned to trim and bind into agonized shapes, now mostly run wild or dead.

During the years the place had been used as a hospital, he had turned the ornamental flower beds into vegetable gardens. His greenhouses forced hothouse tomatoes and melons for the dying patients. Now he tended the place mostly out of love, or the memory of love.

Neither of my parents knew what a superb gardener he was; they only complained about the cost (though he charged for part-time work and supplemented his income doing odd jobs and caretaking for several other summer residents).

Darla joined us when she was out of bed, not because she loved gardening but to be close to me. She was pale and, with her singed and cropped hair, looked touched in the head. She would sit at the edge of a flower bed, pulling up tufts of grass and watching. Sometimes she would wander away a few yards and stare at the ocean or at one of the contorted cedars that separated the grounds from the dunes along the shore.

Dedankalus was kind to her because (this is what I believe) she reminded him of the patients who had once lived in the house and similarly spent their wan convalescence watching him garden.

It was on one of these hot working days, while Dedankalus and I sweated in the rock garden below the back patio, that Billy came home on leave from the army base in Georgia where he was stationed. He was twenty-two, fearful of ghosts, in awe of and hating his father. He wore jeans, a dirty t-shirt, a wallet on a chain and down-at-heel cowboy boots.

. . .

These memories are painful, let me tell you.

And I would not write them out this way except on the advice of my therapist who has come to understand that I cannot speak about what I feel but that I can hint at it in my art or in a diary that will be destroyed, in letters that will not be sent or in stories that will not be read.

The secret self is the real self, and I make my paintings difficult to understand because I am afraid that what I really have to say will be met with apathy and stony silence or a sigh and a quick change of subject. This would be devastating — so I make difficulty the subject of my paintings. The images adumbrate a soul whose unique activity is concealment. It is highly adept, it has made an art, a whole aesthetic out of concealment while yearning, aching, straining for some other connection.

"Why did you let them rob you?" asks Darla.

I don't know what she means.

I am the empty man. I have no feelings left because my habit of concealment has hidden me from myself.

When I started therapy, she said, "This will do you good only if you don't turn it into another technique."

Remembering Billy makes me think of Vicky — the truth is I fell in love with both of them because they rejected me. In bed at night, Vicky would hiss at me in the dark, "Faggot! Queer! Shit-lover! Art-fraud! How many times did you take it up the ass today?" and I would spurt come on my pyjamas, weeping and melting at the same time.

Then she would come by herself, shouting "Mama? Mama? Save them! Can't you save them?"

What she meant by this was a mystery.

That summer, working with Dedankalus, watching his rough hands delve in the soil and fondle the tender plants, watching him casually raise his rifle to kill small animals (so cold and stiff within minutes), observing him unzip his pants and urinate in the junipers, being aware of the ghosts or the sense that always there was someone watching and so much was hidden, I began to have sexual feelings that seemed unconnected with any particular person.

I began to masturbate out of doors, hidden in the dunes, or in the old sanatorium morgue, imagining someone tall and lank and beautiful coming upon me like that, stripping and joining me on the dune grass or the loose cool soil or on the padded gurney.

One day Billy did find me, or (and this is what I think) perhaps he had been watching me all along and only chose then to reveal himself. I pulled up my shorts and started to weep with embarrassment. When I tried to run away, he grabbed my shirt, tearing a button off, and laughed.

It was strange to see him laugh, a combined grimace and sneer. I could see the self-loathing in his face, the compulsion to do the worst thing, to seek danger, to put himself in jeopardy. His carelessness propelled him into some zone of freedom, and our sex became a composition of fear, violence and abandonment.

It was Billy who told us stories about the men and women who haunted the rooms of the old house, about the doomed patients, old and young, or the young nurses recruited with danger pay to care for them, who, as often as not, fell stricken with the same disease and died on the premises. About the babies born to patients lonely for love, babies born with the disease, who died almost at once, buried without names. About the doctors who lived in cottages in the village, their uproarious, drunken parties, their balls, their black-tie bridge tournaments.

It was Billy who told us about St. John Waring's mistress and her apartment over the garage, who showed us the machinery beneath the garage floor that turned the cars around.

Nights, Billy told us, his father had trundled the plain pine
coffins from the morgue and buried them in the lonely, unmarked
graves. It was the memory of this time, of all the anonymous dead,
that had rendered him so inward, silent and cruel. The gardener
had a recurring dream, that he awoke tied up, wrapped in a sheet,
cradled in the frozen earth. A gaunt, skeletal man with red cheeks
and shining eyes bends over and beckons him.

Old Dedankalus had finally married one of the patients, that was
the romance of Billy's life. She was a fortyish, unmarried Italian
woman from New York who had come to the island to die. No one
had ever visited her, so Dedankalus had brought her fresh vegetables
and flowers smuggled from his hothouses. When she was allowed
outside, he would wheel her invalid chair to the row of contorted
trees, explaining about the shapes and the Japanese gardener.

She had died a week after Billy was born, and Dedankalus had
dug her grave.

Billy showed us her admission forms, her death certificate, and,
most chillingly, her autopsy report. He even had a chest x-ray,
showing the lesions and scars on her lungs, the enlarged heart, the
tangle of arteries like the contorted limbs of her husband's trees.

His mother, Billy believed, haunted the house, and whenever I
or Darla came across one of the ghosts (in time, it seemed, we saw
them as often as real people — they grew to accept us and went
about their business as though we weren't there), he would
cross-examine us, hoping that we had spotted her.

I never told him about the woman in the linen closet the day I
found the piece of the True Cross. With those eyebrows and the
pale, gaunt cheeks, they could have been twins.

The worst is that this will go on and on without changing, that my
father's heavy, depressive presence and Mother's melodrama will
define me to eternity. I am happy only when I can lose myself in my

paintings, which are really nothing more than elaborate messages, as Darla says, to the world outside.

It is as if the paintings are myself, and I am this oddly constructed and inept instrument for expressing them. Yet I also stand in the way of my paintings; yes, it is I who obstruct, inhibit, corrupt and deform them.

For me, the task was always to liberate myself from love.

3

DARLA TELEPHONED ME at my loft a week ago.

This was twenty years to the day (I checked the wall calendar next to the phone) since she and Billy tried to elope, stealing his father's car and driving as far as the ferry landing before my father and the gardener caught up with them.

"Why did you let them rob you?" she asked. Perhaps, I thought, she is only asking herself, though she seems to have everything any normal person could desire.

Hearing her voice, I remembered Father, Billy and Vicky and all the other losses and betrayals that seem to comprise my destiny.

One day Billy said to me, "The minute someone tells me he loves me, I start planning my escape as if he had taken me prisoner of war."

"I didn't say I loved you," I pleaded, but by then it was too late.

Sometimes out of loneliness I would crawl into bed with Darla in the mornings, and she would be fully dressed, the ankles of her jeans damp with sand and dew from the dunes.

Sand everywhere.

. . .

Darla had finally talked Mother into letting us sell the Waring place. She wanted me to drive up with her to meet the real estate agent, who was, it turned out, a cousin of Dedankalus.

She went on in a tone of voice I found surprising but also oddly familiar, a tone that was at once breathless and frightened.

Without pausing, she told me that Tad had gone into a corporate drug rehab clinic near Lake Placid, that Lonny, her youngest, her baby, was having nightmares, horrid dreams of dark men cutting off his genitals and throwing him off buildings, that her own life was falling apart. She had had two abnormal pap smears in a row and was scheduled for a biopsy. No one else knew.

After a moment's hesitation, I said yes, remembering the way she looked in the weeks after the lightning struck, her pale vacantness, her cropped hair and the outsized clothes she borrowed from me or Billy.

I said I would pick her up with the boys in the morning. We would make a family outing, complete with a picnic lunch and seafood dinner at Renaldo's on the ferry pier. I would pack the picnic, she should bring the wine from Tad's cellar.

"Don't pretend," she whispered. "You can't even take care of yourself. This terrifies you."

I hung up, wishing she did not know me quite so well.

I thought, these things that happen to us have no cause nor reason. It is as though we are not real at all but being written by some ghostly hand. There is no presence, only a vast nostalgia and, on every page, just the shadow of something which never appears and is never named.

I could not paint any more, just stared and stared at my canvas, a black vortex of images, falling boys, a bloated face covered with moth-like twists of gauze, Japanese screens, bowling pins, a jagged crucifix of light, a girl with blazing hair, Billy Dedankalus slumped in his chair with his rifle propped against his forehead, the way we found him, and myself as a grown man, standing to one side, watching in horror.

That night the black dog visited, by which I mean that I dreamt of Sukey, the gardener's aged black Lab. Waking, I heard the distant rumble of a thunder storm, an occurrence which, for obvious reasons, always sets me on edge. Though it was three a.m., I tried to telephone Darla and kept getting a recorded message telling me to hang up and dial again.

We made the trip in silence.

I asked Darla once when Tad was coming back and then tried to remind her of Mr. La Douceur and his mother's ashes. But she was lost in thought, her fingers working nervously at her pocketbook. She was wearing jeans and one of her husband's checked work shirts. Her hair was done up at the back in a ponytail — such informality has long been completely out of character for her. The boys, in the back seat, seemed crabby and tired and fell asleep before we left the city.

Ray Dedankalus, the cousin, met us at the ferry dock and drove with us to the house, stopping for hamburgers along the way.

Darla maintained her reserved silence, staring out the passenger window. I could not help wondering if, somehow, she were reliving those long ago events. After all, she had driven this road with Billy the night they tried to escape, only to be dragged back from the pier in Old Dedankalus's car. Billy had ridden just ahead of her in the back seat of Father's station wagon.

She remembered Father driving exceedingly slowly all the way back to the house, sometimes stopping for minutes at a time, then jerking forward again. She had had the feeling, she said, that something terrible, something truly evil, was taking place in that station wagon. And she strained her eyes in the dark for any sign of movement. But there was none. The car would stop and then creep forward.

In the morning, we found him dead.

"How did they know?" she wailed. "How did they know?"

I shrugged helplessly and burst into tears at the sight of Billy's body slumped over the rifle.

When we pulled into the drive of the Waring place finally, the boys leaped out and ran ahead, rested, excited to be out of the car, taking turns pretending to be accident victims needing an ambulance. We shook hands with Dedankalus and told him to give us a few hours to look around.

I went to switch on the lights and returned to find Darla gone, the boys shying rocks at the water just past the line of contorted cedars. When I was a boy, the place had seemed big enough to get lost in, much too big for us. Now it startled me how little had changed, with the smell of decay everywhere, the crumbling gatehouse, the dried-up lawn and peeling paint and the ivy growing across the windows so that the rooms were suffused with a dim, green glow.

I thought, if there are ghosts, this is somehow what they must feel, as though they inhabited a reality more vivid, familiar and substantial than themselves.

I called Darla's name and went hunting over the grounds, past the tennis courts and octagonal garage and through the greenhouses now open to the elements and littered with shattered glass. Old Dedankalus's cactus pots still crowded the wooden tables, but nothing grew in them. The earth was desiccated, cracked.

They had buried Billy in a regular graveyard, not on the grounds. We weren't allowed to attend the funeral. Darla stole a bottle of bourbon from Father's cabinet, and we drank it in her room till night came and we knew everything was finished.

"How did they know?" she asked again and again. Though I believe the truth had already begun to clarify itself like muddy water gradually becoming clear as the sediment settles.

. . .

I found Darla in the morgue, now used as a store room for years of accumulated summer furniture, boxes of Christmas ornaments abandoned when we no longer put up a tree, stacks of Father's business records in exploding file boxes, trunks bursting with childhood toys and old photographs — all the detritus of a family we no longer remembered, no longer felt part of. She was leafing through a photograph album, which she held up as I walked in.

"Do you remember the puppy you had when you were three?"

I shook my head, feeling the weight of all the things I did not remember. She jabbed a finger at a snapshot of a smiling toddler struggling to hold a miniature dachshund in his pale arms. The dog has a sharp, wet nose and charming little eyes fixed knowingly on the boy's face.

"You only had him a couple of months. Daddy couldn't stand the noise and the mess."

"I don't remember," I said. "I look happy, though."

"Mama called him Romeo. But you couldn't say that. When you said it, it came out Vemeo." Her face had gone dead, expressionless, yet there was a steely desperation underneath, a determination to assert the truth at any cost.

I handed her back the album and began rummaging, finding a torn Bloomingdale's bag with our remaining croquet mallets and, at the bottom, the plaque that once held a chip of wood from the True Cross. Someone had sawn through the plastic to remove the relic. There was only an empty space where it had been.

"You must remember the night Romeo shit on your bed and Daddy kicked him around the room till he couldn't walk and then said he was taking him to the vet. It was after midnight. We never saw him again."

"I don't remember much," I said.

. . .

But I did remember the morning Billy Dedankalus died.

It was in this very room, the place of the dead, that we found him, purely by chance, since no one yet knew he was missing, and we only came here to hide out. It was our secret place, which, of course, Billy knew.

He had shot himself with the gardener's rifle, nestling the muzzle in the soft V of flesh just beneath his chin and firing up through the back of his mouth into the brain.

Blood had drained from his throat and mouth, soaking his t-shirt and jeans and pooling beneath the chair. But his face was unmarked and bore, partly because of the wide-open eyes, an expression of mild astonishment.

Darla dropped to her knees in the blood and gagged and tried to embrace him, and he fell over onto the floor, awkwardly, like a marionette. The impact of his fall compressed his chest, forcing air suddenly out his lungs, so that he sighed, or seemed to sigh.

Or maybe this was my imagination.

Darla's teeth began to chatter, an inhuman rattle. And I noticed that she was staring into the shadows beyond the x-ray frame.

There seemed to be something there, a shadow within a shadow, a trace of movement.

I don't know now what I saw. But everything had taken on an air of seeming, and what was real was Billy and the blood and the details of the hole in his throat which I have never forgotten — the jagged line of skin, yellow fat, darkening clots of blood, that awful exhalation of breath, as though he had been waiting for us.

I was only thirteen.

I went down beside Darla and tried to touch her, not to comfort her but to try to stop that chattering, which I knew would drive me insane. She mistook my motive and grasped my hand and began to weep, smearing me with blood.

From where I knelt I could finally see what she saw, the gaunt face in the shadows, the pale dome of the woman's forehead above her charcoal eyebrows, her fevered eyes darting with anguish, tears glittering on her cheeks, her silent chest heaving.

As soon as I saw her, she began to fade, her eyes fixed on Billy. Love and pain fused in that look. I have never been able to separate them. There is no such thing as love without betrayal. You hold the thing that kills you as close as you can and watch it die, all the time whispering, Love me, love me, don't go.

Darla took my hand and pressed it.

But her voice was harsh, that tone of desperation. It rasped out the words.

I said nothing. I meant my silence as a confession. Her words were like a burst of light. I held the empty plaque in my hands. Her words went through me like blue fire. Choked with sadness, I remembered how she had looked with her smouldering hair and burned bedclothes.

But I quickly realized that whatever I had to confess was old news. Now she was going to die, and the story had taken on fresh meaning because, like Billy Dedankalus, her boys would always be alone.

We were in the morgue, and I suddenly felt like the only living creature in a room littered with corpses. I stumbled about among the corpses looking for signs of life.

I said nothing — more confession, it was pouring out of me, meaningless. I wanted to weep, but it came out a dry sob. For ages, I have been all dried up inside. I thought what I always think, How am I going to get through this? How am I going to endure such pain? It seems impossible that a human being could suffer this much and live. And just when you think you can't stand any more, it gets worse and you discover new possibilities of living.

This is the reason I have never owned a gun. There is only one person I would shoot and, like my father, I have always found it easy to kill.

Telling it, remembering the intensity, it seems impossible that we could get out of that room alive, that the ordinary world would let us back in. But Darla finally let go of my hand, and her voice began to return to normal. And the past receded until it was nothing but a presence and a dull ache, like a tumour.

I dropped the plaque to the floor. We had somehow agreed to take nothing, to leave everything for the next owner to deliver to the holocaust.

On the stairway, Darla paused. We were brother and sister again, leaving the intolerable splendour of the scene in the morgue for a lesser ecstasy.

She said, "I haven't seen them for years."

I nodded.

"But Lonny does. They're in his dreams."

I shuddered and glanced back, praying for a sight that would sear my eyelids shut forever, but the room was empty.

There was nothing there, nothing as terrible as the future.

Sixteen Categories of Desire

MAMA SAY THERE AIN'T but one desire which is the desire for Our Lord pure and simple. She go up the steps on her face, slowly, slowly, dragging her oxygen bottle, clinkety-clink, while I smoke cigarettes at the top and watch her crawl. Sometime it rain and I still watch her crawl all the way. Then we light candles and inspect the crutches they say got left by other crawlers the Lord cured and Mama claim she feel better and we take the bus home. Though even before we get home, she complain the light hurt her eyes again and pull out the dark glasses and begin to cough and her hand go wrinkle, wrinkle on account of the pain and the bus gas she say is coming up through the floor boards (it a good thing I never listen at the church to throw away that oxygen tank). She always like this, but she proud and still walk to the elevator all dirty wet down her front from crawling up the steps saying she, all in all, feel better. I let her go up on her own with God (though she and He always have a bad time with the lock and sometimes I find her laying down on the floor going flippy-flop like a fish). I stay outside in the cold rain and smoke another cigarette watching the street lights come on and the dirty wet houses opposite where I sometime see a face at a window looking sad. One time I see a naked girl press her whole body against the window.

. . .

Bennett, across the street, is Mama's age, sixty-five, and rich as rich, but he's sick in the heart and lungs. Every day he walk by our place, slow and careful, holding his chest in front like a basket of eggs. He always carry a lit cigarette in his hand, his face look like window putty. Six or seven steps back come his nurse, Grace Mules. She also carry a cigarette in her hand but she get to smoke hers. Sometime Mama and I stroll over to Bennett's to play cribbage. Grace Mules sit in the next room where she keep an eye on him through the door and watch the big screen TV with earphones. Bennett sit across from Mama, a glass of whisky and soda untouched at his elbow, his grey face never move as he wonder over the cards. I always want him to touch me under the table, put his fingers up my skirt. It make me faint to think about. I ask Mama she in love with Bennett. She say she only love the Lord and Bennett too sick to want anything. He want it but he can't have it, I say. Down the street there a woman who had a coke addict for a husband. He went to a party and got coked up and knock his head against a table and die in bed with her that night. Sometime I can't stand to be so close to Bennett, I walk out and stroll down the street. I ask Mama did she love Papa. She say no. Did he see you naked? I ask. He never saw me naked. I let him do it under the covers and only lifted my shift high enough so he could put it in. I am almost fainting when she tell me. I stroll up a street wanting some man to come out of a dirty wet house and do me. I walk past where the girl pressed herself against the window, past the coke widow's green door.

I remember Sister Mary Buntline taught us catechism and the Lord's Prayer in Sunday school at St. Malachy's of Gull Lake and counted out sixteen categories of desire like so many demons meant to drag a body into the Pit of Hell. When I was twelve, she show me the little whippy thing she use to punish herself for bad thoughts. She say I need one too because I have bad thoughts. How you know

I have bad thoughts? I ask. She say everybody have bad thoughts. She have a red face and talk no end about the sixteen categories of desire and take me skinny dipping in Dog Creek and teach me to smoke. I say, What are the sixteen categories of desire? And she say, The first bad category of desire is the desire to have a baby with a man. And the second is to put warm peeled carrots up your ass when you come. She laugh, laugh. And the third is to learn to French inhale when you smoke a cigarette. And the fourth is martyrdom. And the fifth is to relieve yourself in public. She laugh then she start to weep in her hands. Her breath blow in and out and she say, Now touch me there and I'll do you. She say, I'll need the whippy thing tonight. Surely, I say.

Mama she on her knees the whole time we in church. She small and got skin like white paper hanging from her bones. I say, Mama, the Lord got no time for anyone else He have to listen to you so much. She pale and shaky and say she dream of dying every night, that or fornication. She say, I got to pray the sin out. I say, Mama, I don't want no dreams about it, I want a man to do me. She look as if I slap her. She embarrass the priest when she fall on her face on the floor with her arms stretch out. The priest think Mama belong with the Protestants. He think Mama got too much desire for the Lord. I know he think that nobody got that much desire for the Lord and probably anybody act up like Mama and say it for the Lord really mean she need to get done or turn Protestant. When she with Bennett, she drink ice tea and come over all girlish, which I know don't mean nothing because she never wanted to get done even by Papa. She just act like she want to get done then start to cough and complain of the light and she shut herself in her room at home and I hear the swish, swish of the prayers rising. We go back to the steps. She take three hours crawling up in the rain, make herself sick. I get flirty with priests, maintenance men and penitents crawling the

steps on their knees, sitting with my skirts up and smoking cigarettes. Sister Mary Buntline say the sixth category of desire is for
forced sex with large numbers of muscular black men. And the
seventh is to run away to Arkansas to join the snake handlers in
order to experience the grace of God in this life in an atmosphere of
polyester coordinates and primitive country rock music. And the
eighth is for hard cylindrical objects. And the ninth is for World
Peace and an end to the slaughter of dolphins. And the tenth is to
commit violent atrocities against those weaker than ourselves. And
the eleventh is for things to be nice. She screw up her red face and
say maybe that the worst of all. Then she say sometime she just
want, not even knowing what she want, that she want only to submit
to the wanting, just say to life anything any way and close her eyes.
And now when I remember this, I think of that girl with her body
pressed up against the window glass for all the world to see.

Mama, I say one time, why it so hard to get a man to do you? Seem
like it ought to be a simple thing. Say come here fella and bathe me
in your jets of sperm. Mama pretend she don't hear me. And I ain't
found a man yet man enough to respond to that particular request.
I miss Sister Mary Buntline, who would be laughing now. She say
her snatch was a miracle, the eighth effing wonder of the world and
a proof of God. I say, Mama, Sister Mary Buntline some kind of
saint. And Mama sniff and say Sister Mary Buntline end up
married to a ex-priest named Leonard Malfy and three rat-face
apostate children running a AIDS clinic in Seattle. Boys, I say, that
sure sound bad all right. Sound like Hell on earth. It sound like
pure-d evil all right. Jesus. Married with kids and a job. What sane
decent woman would want that? Why I bet she don't get poke
more than once a night. How she stand it? Shut up, say Mama.
That ain't all. She dead now. That stump me. I never know she was
dead. Mama got a wicked smile on her face so I know it must be

true. Sister Mary Buntline the only person I ever love. One time she say, pausing with her finger up my ass, she recall a nuns' vacation to Disneyland — eight penguins with PMS in a Dodge minivan with the AC on the fritz. And she slip away and rent a red convertible with the convent credit card and drag her favourite t-shirt over her bikini and head for the beach with the words THE BEST LITTLE FUCK IN TOWN across her chest, a carton of American Spirit cigarettes and a bottle of Jose Cuervo on the seat beside her, and the Rolling Stones shrieking out the tape deck. She laugh, laugh like that. I don't understand a word she say. Except, she tell me, that when the Mother Superior give her the whippy thing to punish herself. How she die? I ask Mama, never wanting to hear a answer. In the sea, she say. The ocean. Maybe she kill herself because of that no good husband. Maybe she just walk in cause of all the evil she done. Or maybe the hand of God come out of a wave and grab her off the beach. No, I say. Maybe it only look like she die. Maybe God send down a vehicle that look like it come out of the sea. Maybe she in Heaven looking down at us right now. Mama sniff and say she thinking about the steps again. Surely, I say.

Sister Mary Buntline say we always falling in love with people we got nothing in common with except the desire to get done. She say the pussy named like the moon or the stars. Mons Veneris, Labia Minoris, Labia Majoris, clitoris, vulva. That a kind of car I say. She laugh, laugh and hold me close. She say the twelfth category of desire is for warm golden memories of early years on the family farm, of social success in high school, of fashion triumphs, of dates with virile yet innocent football players, of joining the cheer leading squad in senior year. And the thirteenth is to get tied up, spanked and peed on. I say Mama say Immaculate Conception the best thing God invented. Sister Mary Buntline laugh and remember a sign she see in Bogue Chitto where she grew up. It say, Onan Generators. It another thing God invented, she say. She say when she eighteen she had a call to join the Sisters of Egregious Affliction. Who call? I ask. No one, she say sadly. It the fourteenth category of desire.

Bennett croak one night just about sunset when the light burst through the rain clouds a moment and the street shine all way down to the jetties on Lake Pontchartrain. Bennett go down and they arrest Grace Mules. She walk to the police car with a cigarette in her mouth and her wrists cuffed in front of her. She don't look whichaway except once, as she get in the car, she look up at our windows. I say, Mama, why she kill old Bennett? Mama say nothing. She never even look out the window when they take Bennett's body out in a bag. I say, You think she kill him out of pity? Mama, she in love with old Bennett or something? Mama sniff. I think she about to cry on account of missing cribbage with Bennett but she got this look on her face, a terrible look I never see before, like she about to pop, like she win something big. I say, Mama, Mama, you tell me, tell me now. But I already know because of that look. I say, Mama, she love old Bennett didn't she? All this time she his nurse and his lover. And she get jealous of you and Bennett playing cribbage every night. Maybe Bennett going to fire her or something because she don't want you coming over. Maybe it all about sex, Mama. Only sex don't mean nothing to you do it? Because you don't want to get done. You just come over all girly girl with Bennett out of spite. Mama's face look like it going to burst. She start to cough and she all red like she going to explode. She make a sign that she want her oxygen bottle but I hold it away from her. I say, Sister Mary Buntline tell me about this. She say the fifteenth category of desire is the petty cruelty of the weak and the disappointed. Mama gasping for breath now but defiant. In the street Grace Mules cast her eyes up at our windows. The cop follow her eyes and wonder what she thinking. The naked girl watch the red and blue police lights from behind her curtains. The coke widow crouch behind her door. Mama close her eyes and whisper yes.

I take care of Mama after what happen, after we leave Gull Lake and all. I never hear from Sister Mary Buntline, never a letter or a call. I don't know if she embarrassed or if maybe it hurt so much she can't bear to be reminded. Sometime I think the church lock her up in a little cell in the basement with water on the floor and rats hip-hopping around. She just naked there with a chain around her neck and her whippy thing for company. But then Mama tell the story about how she marry Leonard Malfy and get swallowed up in the sea one day. I say, Mama, how come I got to take care of you and you my Mama and all and should be taking care of me. She say it love that make me do it. She say she already give and give so much there ain't anything left and now it my turn to give and give. That what God want. I say, I don't recall the part where you give and give. Was that before I was born? She say she give too much and my ingratitude a proof of that. She say she don't deserve half the things that happen to her. I say, I don't recall anything happening to you, Mama, anything it all. Mama clap her hands over her ears. I say, I never know a person keep herself so safe from things happening. She say, You are trying to kill me. I say, Sister Mary Buntline just the opposite she always praying Lord make something happen to me right here in St. Malachy's of Gull Lake, make something happen, a miracle or a orgasm or anything else, just so I don't go to bed tonight thinking nothing happen to me today. She say, Don't save me, Lord, just use me up, just use me up so there nothing left when I die. I say, Maybe that why she do me and marry Leonard Malfy and have three kids and walk into the sea.

· · ·

We at the steps again. She go up on her face and hands, slowly, slowly, dragging her oxygen bottle. The dome at the top look like Sister Mary Buntline's left tit. I smoke an American Spirit cigarette I got off a black woman name Charnese who sell Sacred Heart key chains in the souvenir shop. Mama gathering a crowd on account of her slow and painful progress in the rain. People in the crowd think Mama a saint or something on account of the struggle she have getting up the steps and the way she snarl at a man who offer to help her. Pretty soon she got half a dozen men and women on their faces crawling behind her. A priest come by and try to get people to go about their business but then he watch Mama for a while, her face blue and frothy on account of I put a empty oxygen bottle in her bag when we left home. Mama resting with her cheek on the dirty step. The priest offer to get her a stretcher or a wheel chair but she ignore him and start crawling. Mama got tears in her eyes or maybe it just rain. The priest start to weep too and make the sign of the cross over Mama and kneel beside her. He join the crawlers going slowly, slowly up the steps. It a big day for Mama only I don't think she know it. She got her eye on the dome at the top and not the crowd of crawlers behind her or the ambulance they got waiting or the TV crew with big lights on dollies or the sisters saying their beads on the terraces ahead of her or the big red-faced policemen in orange slickers holding umbrellas over her. And it scare me how quiet everything become with all that crowd and only the snap, snap of flashbulbs going off and the clinkety-clink of the oxygen bottle as she drag it up.

Some boys find us down at Dog Creek one day. I don't know how they find us. One name of Kittery used to like me and grab my titties when we play fox and hounds. Sister Mary Buntline say run, run. We stretch out naked on a rock smoking and drinking wine she steal from the priest's locker and she jump up and run and shout for me to run. I try to run but Kittery catch me by the foot and kick me off the rock. I screaming and splashing in the shallows with my arm broke and the boys gather round and start in with their boots. Kittery take off his belt and whip the buckle over his head and blood pops out of me and little tore corners of skin. He can't stand me looking and put his boot over my face till my nose crack and I start to drown. He jump on the rock and drop a stone. My eye feel like they poke a red-hot stick in and jumble it around. I think it funny I ain't dead when I hurt so much. Then Sister Mary Buntline kneeling over me. It a little hard to see her through one eye and it not working too well but I never see a body so white and trembling and my blood drenched down her front and she praying and crying and cursing and saying she sorry all at once and trying with her fingers to make my face look like a face again. Then she scoop me in her arms like a baby and walk back to Gull Lake. She walk straight up the street with me in her arms naked, bloody, not looking like anything human. People in the street stare, traffic stop, nobody help. Papa run to meet us at the yard gate and take me himself. But Mama at the door screaming I won't have that in my house get it away from here it make me sick it make me want to puke it a abomination it a thing, and she collapse on the step. Papa look helpless. I can see how he is thinking life ain't been too good lately and all the women around, the ones who supposed to love him and make him feel like something, just pure hateful, and he do the only manly thing which is drop me on the grass and fetch his straight razor from the bathroom shelf and shout, Is this what you want? Is this what you want? and cut his own throat right there in front of the whole town and Mama and me and Sister Mary Buntline.

· · ·

After Gull Lake Mama get the wander bug only she don't know it. We go settle for good in Eastabuchie where she got relatives. Then we settle for good in Red Lick, Hopewell and Hot Coffee which is all black people and seem like a bad idea from the start. In Ragged Point Mama hear about the steps. Everywhere we go I miss Sister Mary Buntline. I miss her red face and sighs and the way she laugh when she tickle me. One time she sit with me in the pines behind St. Malachy's of Gull Lake spying on the sisters. She say there go Sister Theresa of the Screaming Orgasms and there go Mother Mary of the Silent Masturbators and there go Our Father Confessor of the Inexplicable Erections. She laugh, laugh and say her body a temple come and worship. Surely, I say. She say the Lord invented the orgasm so people would make babies but it one of those inventions that got away from Him. Once she come to visit me in the hospital, the last time I see her. She kiss me on the lips which hurt like Hell but I love the hurt. She lean over and whisper in my ear. She say there a country called Tibet where they write prayers on pieces of paper and set fire to the paper and the smoke carry the prayers up to heaven. She say the sixteenth bad category of desire is the desire for Our Lord pure and simple. But, she say, there ain't no end to desire. She say the Maya kings used to slash their penises and wash their alters in blood. She say there a country called Peru where once they strangled children and left them on mountaintops. And in ancient Carthage they threw infants into the fires of Baal. Because, like us, the gods are insatiable. Life a thing of gorgeous violence and sorrow, she say. It certainly a big surprise to me, I say. Ain't nothing happen yet the way I expect it. Sister Mary Buntline blow through her mouth, start to giggle. But then she stop. Ain't no reason for us, she say, no reason at all, except to burn.

Acknowledgements

"La Corriveau," *Meurtres à Quebec* (Quebec: L'Instant même, 1993); *Descant* (Winter 1993); *94 Best Canadian Stories* (Ottawa: Oberon, 1994).

"A Piece of the True Cross," *Paper Guitar: 27 Writers Celebrate 25 Years of Descant* (Toronto: HarperCollins, 1995).

"State of the Nation," *New Orleans Review* (Summer 1997); *Canadian Fiction* 93-94 (1998).

"My Romance," *Descant* (Spring 1998); *99 Best Canadian Stories* (Ottawa: Oberon, 1999).

"The Left Ladies Club," *Grain* (Spring 1999).

"Abrupt Extinctions at the End of the Cretaceous," *Canadian Forum* (May 1999).

"Lunar Sensitivities," *Descant* (Winter 1999).

"Bad News of the Heart," *The New Quarterly* (2000).

"The Indonesian Client," The International Short Story at the End of the Millenium, *Descant* (2000).